Resilience

Resilience

a collection of stories

by Jim Bates

Bridge House

British Library Cataloguing in Publication Data
A Record of this Publication is available from the British
Library

ISBN 978-1-914199-00-4

This edition published 2021 by Bridge House Publishing
Manchester, England

Cover photograph © Thomas R. Bates

Dedicated to my mom, Betty Ann Cory, who taught me to make the most of life's challenges and to take time to appreciate the beauty in nature.

Contents

Remembrance Day

"Allie, come here, a minute. Look at this," the old man said and pointed. "It's a special kind of wild flower called a trillium."

Intrigued, the little girl ran to his side and fell to her knees, her face only inches from the white petals. "Pretty," she said, and bent closer, pushing her long red hair behind one ear exposing her cheeks dotted with freckles.

"There's usually not much of an aroma," the old man said, as he stiffly got down on the ground, joining his granddaughter. She was wearing yellow and red striped tights under a white and black striped short-sleeve dress covered with pink hearts. On her feet were purple socks and pink tennis shoes.

"But, Grandpa, it smells good," she said, excitedly, moving over to make room for him.

He bent down and took a whiff of the imaginary scent. "Oh, you are right," he agreed, looking with affection at the little girl. "It does smell good."

They were just coming out of a small woodland near a park where they'd been playing on the swings. A moving shadow on the ground caught their attention. The little girl looked up and saw a large bird.

"Crow," she dutifully recited. The old man grinned with the memory of when he'd taught her to not only identify the bird, but also to say its name. Then a sudden movement to the left captured her attention. She turned quickly and spied a robin hoping nearby on a sunlit patch of grass. "Look at that," she said, pointing excitedly. "Rrrrr... rrrr... Robin." She looked at her grandfather and smiled. It was their little joke about how he'd taught her to identify this particular early spring bird and pronounce its name with rolling rs for both robin and red breast.

God, the affection he felt toward this little girl; his son's daughter, the youngest of Steve and his Nora's four kids.

Suddenly nearby a dog yipped. Allie stood up quickly and pointed, "Look Grandpa. A doggy."

He got to his feet and turned. Coming down the street was a lady in a blue sweat suit walking a small white dog that was straining on its leash. "Stand behind me," he said, moving her out of the way, protecting her. As the lady approached, he said politely, "Nice dog you've got there. What kind is it?"

She gave him an odd look, sizing him up before answering, "It's a Westie."

He turned to his granddaughter. "Did you hear that, honey? Can you say Westie?"

Allie didn't answer, only watched shyly as the lady and the dog walked by, hurrying a little it seemed to the old man. He watched until they were out of range and then asked, "Did you like the doggy?"

"I did, Grandpa, I did. He was so cute!" She exclaimed, smiling. "I loved it."

"Maybe someday your mom and dad can get you a doggy," he said, starting to walk down the street toward his son's home.

She reached up and took his hand. "Maybe," she said, sounding unsure. Then she had a thought and visibly cheered. "But, if they don't, will you get one for me, Grandpa? Please?"

He smiled to himself before answering. "Well, it's really up to your mom and dad." Then he glanced at her and seeing the disappointment in her eyes, quickly added, "But, we'll see, sweetheart. We'll see."

"Good," she said, smiling. Then she started humming to herself. The old man didn't recognize the tune, but that was all right. It was just good to be together.

They walked along for half a block taking their time

until Allie let go of his hand and pointed. "Look Grandpa, tulips," she called out. "Come with me. Hurry! "She ran ahead to the next yard.

The old man followed behind, his steps slow but steady. In a minute he caught up to her. She was squatting down, studying the bright spring flower. "Two, two, two lips," he said, pointing to his mouth as he approached her.

She turned and laughed. "No, Grandpa. Tu… lips," she said, emphasizing each of the two syllables. He smiled, remembering how much fun it had been teaching her letters and words throughout her young life. She moved over to a different flower. "Look grandpa, your favourite colour. Orange."

"Yes, it is, honey." Then he paused and rubbed the whiskers on his chin in mock contemplation. "Say, what's your favourite colour again?" he asked, pretending he'd forgotten.

"Purple and pink," she said, standing up and poking at him. "You know that." She giggled and then added, "You're so silly, Grandpa."

They started walking again, her soft, small hand in his large, callused one. She was five years old, average height, and was way too skinny in his estimation, even though she ate well at every meal. She was fun loving and had a unique personality all her own. When they were together they talked and laughed and she was a true joy in his life.

The next house up ahead was his son's home. He pointed. "Let's go into your folk's back yard and play."

"Sure," she agreed and ran off. The old man was eighty-six years old and followed as fast as he could. It took him a while.

A few minutes later his son Steve who was standing at the window and looking into the backyard called to his wife, "There he is, Nora, I see him. There's Dad."

11

"Finally," she said, somewhat annoyed. "He's lived with us for ten years. Today of all days he should know we'd be eating by six o'clock."

Steve checked his wristwatch and said, "He still has a few minutes."

"What's he doing out there anyway?"

"Looks like he's dancing."

"What?"

"Dancing." Steve shook his head grinned to himself. He liked that his father was a bit of an eccentric. It kept things interesting. Most of the time, anyway, but not today. Today was different. "Never mind. I'll go get him."

"Please hurry. I'm putting the food on the table."

In the dining room sat Steve and Nora's other four children. This was the family's Remembrance Day. The day they set aside every year to remember the short life of Alisha Ann Drayton, Steve and Nora's youngest daughter who fifteen years ago today had died at the age of five from acute lymphoblastic leukaemia.

Steve went downstairs and out of the back door. "Hey Dad," he called. "Come on in. Dinner's on the table."

Out in the yard, the old man stopped running around and playing tag with Allie. She was wearing him out and he was getting tired, even though he didn't mind trying to keep up. He just wasn't as young as he wanted to be.

He turned toward his son. "All right. Just give me a minute."

"Sure, Dad," Steve said, walking over. He put his arm affectionately around his father's shoulder. "You doing okay?"

"Yeah, son, I am." He was quiet for a moment. "I just miss her, you know. I miss being with her. Playing with her. We were close. She was one of the best things that ever happened to me." He paused a moment and then added,

"It's not just today, son, but every day. Every day is Remembrance Day. At least it is for me." His eyes suddenly became moist as tears formed.

Steve sighed and gave his dad a compassionate hug. "Me, too, Dad," he said, "me, too."

Then they walked slowly towards the back door. The old man didn't want to go inside just yet, but knew he had to. Nora had dinner ready and he didn't want to be rude. After all, it was generous of his son and wife to have him to live with them. More than generous.

Over his shoulder the old man turned and waved to Allie, standing in the middle of the yard. The wind blew through her hair and the sun caught her freckles just right, making them seem to sparkle. She smiled and waved back, locked forever in the old man's memory.

"I'll see you soon," he said to his granddaughter as he turned and started for the door.

"What'd you say, Dad?" Steve asked.

"Nothing," the old man said. "It must have been the wind."

Then he turned and waved to Allie one more time before finally going inside.

The Rabbit

"I'm going to the compost bin," Blake Jorgenson said to his wife Alicia. "I'll be right back."

"Okay. I'm almost done with the tea. We can have a nice cup on the back patio if you'd like. It's a beautiful morning."

"Sounds great."

Blake stepped out of the back door with his small pail of breakfast scraps: egg shells, a rind of grapefruit and a banana peel. He stopped and took a moment to breathe in the lovely scent of a nearby climbing yellow rose bush. *Ah, roses so sweet,* he thought poetically to himself.

Life was grand and he was feeling wonderful. A house wren chattering happily in a nearby clump of honeysuckle echoed his jaunty mood. Morning dew sparkled on the lawn and the sky was a glorious blue. It was the last week in June, the sun was shining and the temperature a pleasant sixty-five degrees. It was going to be a perfect day.

Blake was an avid gardener; it was not only his hobby but his passion. He planned to spend the morning working in the front yard, weeding and hoeing the many gardens he'd planted over the years. It was the sunniest spot on his property and that's where all the sun-loving flowers were: delphinium, garden phlox, coneflower, sunflowers, daises and black-eyed Susans. When he was finished in the front, he'd move to the backyard, where he was now, to the shady gardens and do the same with the hostas, ferns, wild ginger, Solomon's seal and foxglove. He prided himself on the flowers he and Alicia grew. They'd won a disappointing second place red ribbon in the Orchard Lake garden contest last year, which by his high standards was unacceptable not to mention embarrassing. He was ready to do battle.

He'd announced at the beginning of the season, "This is our year, Alicia. No pathetic second place for us. No siree! This year we're going to step it up a notch. Make no doubt about it. We're going to win."

He hadn't noticed when Alicia turned away, rolling her eyes. Sure, she liked to putter around in the garden. It was good exercise and all that, but she wasn't bothered about the contest and didn't care one whit about winning. And she certainly wasn't like her competitive husband, who had waited and dreamed and plotted all winter long for the chance to wipe last year's second place debacle from the books.

Blake happily sauntered from the back door to the far side of the garage where the compost bin was located. Suddenly, a fleeting motion to his right caught his attention. Thinking it might be a robin searching for a worm he glanced out into the yard. It took a moment but then what he saw made his blood pressure sky-rocket, his good mood vanishing in an instant.

"Oh no!" He dropped his pail and ran back to the house yelling, "God damn it!"

Alicia hurried to meet him as he burst through the backdoor. "What's the matter? Is it your heart? What's wrong?"

"No, it's not my heart," he barked. "I'm fine, but I'm not okay. I've got to call Toby."

"Why?"

"That damn rabbit is back. I can't believe it."

Oh, oh. This isn't good, Alicia thought, remembering back a few years ago. "Why call Toby?" Toby McCourt was Blake's best friend.

"He's got a trap. I'm going to catch the blasted thing and when I do that'll be all she wrote for mister bunny rabbit. Mark my words. That thing is toast."

Alicia sighed a heavy sigh, thinking, *Good grief, here we go again.*

Toby's trap was called a "Havaheart." It was a rectangular wire mesh box-like contraption that an animal was enticed into with food. Once inside, a trip-lever shut the door so the animal couldn't get out. The idea was that the captive could then be taken far away and released to run wild and free in some woods or fields; away from where they could do damage and destruction to humans. Toby used his to trap squirrels. He was a gentle and compassionate man who drove twenty miles to the other side of the Minnesota River where he set the unharmed animal loose. Blake wasn't sure he'd be that kind and considerate with the rabbit.

"I might just drop the whole thing in the middle of Orchard Lake and be done with it," he told Alicia when he returned home from Toby's, hauling the bulky Havaheart. I've had it with that damn thing."

That "Damn Thing," the rabbit, had been the scourge of Blake's for a couple of years right up until last year when it had mysteriously disappeared. "Good riddance," Blake had exclaimed earlier that spring as he prepared his prized gardens for the garden show judging. The rabbit had not appeared all that summer which only made being awarded that gut wrenching second place red ribbon even more infuriating. "Maybe a fox got it or something," he'd said to Alicia at the end of the season. "Hopefully, the stupid thing is dead. Good bye and good riddance is what I say."

Alicia had crossed her fingers, hoping for his sake that her highly strung husband was right, but secretly guessing he wasn't. She'd grown up on a farm and knew animals were often a lot smarter than humans.

Now a year later, it turned out she was unfortunately right. It was obvious that Blake's nemesis was not dead, not even close. It was back, alive and well, hopping around in the yard without a care in the world and it had Blake's blood pressure up in the danger zone.

"Blake, sweetheart, you've got to calm down," Alicia told him, running to keep up as he stalked their property, trap in hand, searching for the perfect place to set it. "You'll give yourself a heart attack."

Blake was a retired product development specialist for Heartland Incorporated, an electronics manufacturing company. He'd worked there for nearly forty years, as long as he and Alicia had been married. He'd been a dedicated employee and was a devoted husband. He was also fiercely competitive, and he wasn't going to let a measly cottontail rabbit ruin his changes at winning first place at garden show this year. In his words, "No bleepin' way." He'd already picked out a nice spot on the fireplace mantel to be home for the shining golden first place trophy, much to Alicia's chagrin.

After an hour stalking back and forth trying various locations, he finally decided to place the trap in the front yard, in the middle of his favourite flower bed. He baited it with fresh romaine lettuce, sliced radishes and succulent baby carrots. The mixture looked so delectable that Blake fought back an urge to eat some. "Nope, save it for the rabbit," he muttered to himself. "I can't wait to get the damned thing."

With the trap and bait in place, he impatiently waited. One day went by. A second day passed. A third. Nothing. At the end of the fourth day, with still no rabbit in sight, Blake was calming down and starting to think, *Maybe the blasted thing has moved on to another neighbourhood to terrorize another gardener.* Or, now that he was thinking about it, *Maybe something even better has happened. Maybe it got hit by a car and is dead.* To that end Blake got

17

in his car and took a drive around the neighbourhood looking up and down the streets to see if he could find evidence of the smashed remains of a rabbit's demise. He found nothing.

But that was fine with Blake. At least the rabbit wasn't in the yard or his flower beds, or anywhere nearby. Apparently. He allowed himself some cautious optimism. His bachelor buttons had just popped up in the front yard garden and were growing with enthusiasm. They'd be the final colours of blue and pink and white to fill in amongst the deep violet delphinium, the terra cotta coneflowers, the yellow sunflowers and the deep fuchsia and reds of his phlox. The judging was next week. He and more importantly, the garden were ready.

"First place, here we come," he told Alicia, "no doubt in my mind." To which his long suffering wife sighed and again rolled her eyes, this time crossing her fingers for luck hoping he was right. It'd certainly make life easier. For both of them.

The next morning he took the breakfast scraps to the compost bin. On a whim, he decided to take a little stroll to the front yard to check on the trap. He walked across yesterday's freshly cut grass and along the side of his house, revelling in the beauty of the natural world and the fact that with the rabbit seemingly nowhere to be found all was right with it. He turned the corner to the front yard and let his eyes run over the riot of colour, the beautiful combination of flowers of all types and varieties. He'd definitely win first place this year. Easily.

Then he happened to glance at the Havaheart, tucked carefully among the bachelor buttons. At first he didn't believe what he saw. He had to blink twice to make sure it was real before realizing that it was. There, sitting calmly and unafraid, on top of the trap was the rabbit. Blake stared, his blood racing to his brain, his heart pounding. He put his hand to his chest to ease a sudden pain. It subsided, fortunately, but he was frozen in place, a combination of disbelief and rage stopping him in his tracks.

The rabbit, a doe, a big female, sat staring back at him, calmly munching on the sweet tasting bachelor buttons growing right beside her. She was taking her time, all the while watching the man clutch his chest, as she munched, munched, munched away, savouring every delicious bite, in no hurry at all.

When she was finished, she jumped to the ground and leisurely hopped away, turning every now and then, keeping an eye on the crazy man with his eyes bugging out, silently moving his mouth, no sound coming out. She spied a delectable delphinium, stopped and daintily bit it off at the stem and started chewing, watching as the female who lived with the man ran out to him.

Alicia had seen the entire episode from the front window and ran out to help. When she got to Blake she could see he was shaken but otherwise all right. She wrapped an arm around his waist and helped him toward the front door. "Let's get you inside, dear. You need to rest. And you especially need to calm down about that rabbit. You're going to give yourself a heart-attack."

Blake begrudgingly accepted his wife's assistance, but he had enough strength to try and argue his point. "Didn't you see it out there? That damn rabbit? Taunting me with those beady little eyes? It was like it was laughing at me. I promise you this, Alicia, I'll never give up. I'll get that rabbit if it's the last thing I do."

Alicia was direct and to the point. "Listen to yourself Blake. You sound like a pouting five year old. Just give it a rest, will you? Put that rabbit out of your mind." She got him settled on the couch and wrapped in a blanket. Then she patted him on the shoulder and kissed his forehead. "You lie here and rest. I'll go make some tea."

Blake closed his eyes. It felt good to be lying down. Now that he thought about it, Alicia was partly right. He should try to relax. But the rest of what she said about putting the rabbit out of his mind? Never. He wasn't done yet. Not by a long shot. *I'll get that rabbit if it's the last thing I do*, he was thinking, just before he drifted off to sleep.

Outside the rabbit hopped through more of the succulent garden, so full of tasty flowers, such good food. For now, though, she ignored them. She was heading for the house next door. At the back of the garage she'd dug a burrow for her nine babies. They'd been born last week and she was still feeding them her rich mother's milk. Soon they'd be old enough to go out on their own. Then she would teach them the ways of the world and how to survive: where the safe places to hide were and where to find food. Like this particular garden, this lovely banquet of healthy greens, so abundant and nutritious.

But that was still a few weeks away. Until then she'd be busy, feeding mostly, both herself and her babies. She was glad there were so many flowers nearby. The man's garden held the best food in the area; in fact, the best food she'd ever eaten. She was sure her babies would grow strong and healthy from it. Her milk was good. The garden was big. The food source was almost unending. There was no doubt about it; she would definitely be back, if not this afternoon, then tonight. After all, she had a growing family to care for. She had a lot more eating to do.

Turok and Andar

"John, you doing all right down there?"

"Yeah," he yelled back upstairs. He really was, even though they were getting ready for his brother's funeral. He flipped open the comic book he'd been looking at, *Turok Son of Stone # 4, The Bridge To Freedom*. The one with Turok on the cover, spear in hand, his brother Andar beside him, holding a club, getting ready to face a huge Tyrannosaurus Rex. "Just thinking about Andy."

He listened to Maggie's soft footsteps on the stairs and in a moment she was standing next to him, hand resting on his shoulder. "You're going to miss him, aren't you?"

John set his comic book aside. Over the years he'd collected all sixteen of the early editions of *Turok Son of Stone*. They were published between 1955 and 1960 and told of the adventures of two young Native American brothers trapped by an earthquake in a canyon in the rugged southwest desert, a treacherous land populated with huge flesh eating dinosaurs. He kept each issue in a plastic sleeve in a dark green three ring binder that now lay open on his desk. He caressed it lightly before closing it. "Yeah, Maggie, I really am."

His wife of forty-one years pulled up a chair, sat next to him and put her hand on his arm. "We can wait a few minutes to leave if you want."

"No, we should get going." He sighed and was quiet for a moment.

"What?"

"I was just thinking about one time up at the lake."

"Up north?"

"Yeah, Aunt Harriet and Uncle David's place on Big Sandy."

"Their summer place, right?" He nodded. "What were you thinking about?"

"Oh, I don't know. Just stupid kid's stuff."

Maggie knew how close John and his brother had been. Andy had died the previous week after a mercifully short struggle in the aftermath of a massive stroke. He'd been sixty-two. John, two years older, had been by his side right up to the very end. She'd never known two people as close as the brothers were. Never. Now John would have to figure out how to move on and live life on his own.

Maggie gently began to rub her husband's shoulder. She'd heard his stories many times but knew he needed to talk. "You always loved it up there, didn't you?"

"Yeah, I did. Both of us." He sighed and fought back a tear.

John had hundreds of stories about "Being at the Lake," as he called those times. Today, the one he told Maggie went like this:

"It was mid-afternoon in early August. White caps were marching across the big lake, waves crashing on the shore. The wind was blowing hard off the water cooling the two brothers as they played in the shade of a huge cottonwood tree in the front yard. Auntie Harriet had let them use an old quilt and they'd spread it out on the lawn.

" 'This will be our raft,' John had said.

" 'We'll be on the ocean,' Andy added, beginning to embellish the imaginary game they were creating at just that very moment.

" 'I'll be Turok and…'

" 'I'll be Andar,' Andy grinned.

"In the comics, Turok was the older brother and Andar the younger one, a relationship that worked perfectly for both boys.

"John shaded his eyes with his hand, peering out in front

22

of them. 'Let's try to paddle across to the other side. See if we can find some food. We can hunt for some Pterodactyl eggs or something.'

" 'Oh, boy, Turok, these waves are huge,' Andy said, looking worried. 'Do you think we can make it?' He began bouncing up and down on his knees, mimicking a treacherous crossing.

" 'Yeah, we can,' John said, simulating paddling and stroking mightily. 'We just have to keep our eyes peeled and watch out for sea monsters.'

"For a minute the brothers were silent, each bouncing on their knees as they paddled across their make believe ocean, both of them lost in their own world.

"Suddenly Andy yelled, 'Turok, watch out.' He lunged for his brother and pulled him down on the raft, covering him with his body, protecting him. 'That huge water dinosaur almost got you.'

" 'Oh, boy, that was close,' John said, sitting up and wiping his brow. 'Thanks, Andar, I'm safe now.'

"The two brothers smiled at each other and began paddling again."

The scene played out in John's mind as he told the tale to his wife, missing nothing, the memory as fresh as the day it happened, over fifty years ago.

When he finished talking he became quiet. Maggie, who had been rubbing his shoulder the entire time, squeezed it and stood up. "I should probably finish getting ready." She looked at the clock on the wall. "The service starts in just over an hour."

"Yeah, I know. I'll be ready. We can leave in ten minutes."

"Okay. See you upstairs?"

"Yeah, I'll be there."

John watched Maggie walk up the steps, then sat for a

minute, thinking of his brother and how the term 'missing him' would never begin to describe what he was going through. They had been so close. There were so many good memories.

After they had reached adulthood, John became a high school science teacher while Andy worked in construction, framing homes for a local contractor. They'd stayed in touch, calling each other every day or so and getting together at least once a week. Their wives became friends, and even their kids got along. Their lives had been rich and fulfilling though they'd each battled their own personal demons, John with alcohol, Andy with pain killers. Even during those difficult years, though, they'd managed to find a way to stay in contact. In many ways, they were more than brothers, they were best of friends; soul mates.

And that's why it was frustrating, sometimes, to try to explain how much Andy's loss meant. In John's mind's eye he saw Andy back at Big Sandy Lake on their raft, battling the waves, fighting the good fight against water monsters and dinosaurs, his skin tanned chestnut brown from weeks in the sun.

They only wore cut-off jeans those summers, no shirts or shoes. The air smelled of lake, a perfume of rotting seaweed and dead fish only eleven and nine year old boys could appreciate, even love. The sun was always shining, the sky azure blue with white puffy clouds drifting by and purple martins calling in the background, nearly drowned out by the squawking of the gulls forever flying overhead.

In the early evening the two of them fished from the dock, casting their lines, the lake turning still as the sun went down, the water smoothing to glass, water bugs skating across the surface as a yellow moon rose above the trees to the east. A little while later the Milky Way would then magically appear, stars covering the domed sky in a whitewash of cosmic beauty.

Even now, at the time of Andy's death, John sober for fifteen years, Andy drug free for fourteen, the memories of those long ago days were as fresh and clear as they had been back then, the pure unencumbered days of their youth.

John sat quietly for a moment. He knew he should get going. Knew he should take the next step towards laying his brother to rest and moving forward with the rest of his life. But he wasn't ready. Instead, he reached for his binder. It opened arbitrarily to *Turok and Andar # 16, Secret Of The Giants*, the first of the comics he'd ever purchased when he'd started collecting them. It had the two brothers on the cover, bow and arrows in their hands, facing a Stegosaurus, ready to fight to the death.

John smiled and opened the comic to the first page and began to read. The clock on the wall inched forward but the service could wait. His brother was still with him. He wasn't ready to say good-bye just yet.

Planes Overhead

The temperature was in the low forties, the first really warm day after a long cold winter. My wife Elise wanted to spend some time with our eldest daughter, so I dropped her off at Emily's house and went to nearby Lake Harriet, one of the city's most charming lakes, to hang out for a while. I sat on a park bench in the sun watching the world go by: young couples strolling hand in hand, grinning silly grins, head over heels in love; parents pushing strollers with their new born child bundled safely inside; kids running and joyfully stomping in slushy puddles of melting snow, parents smiling and making no attempt to stop them; old folks taking their time, walking slowly, enjoying the pleasant day. All of it good. All of it uplifting. But, if that were the case, then why did I feel so melancholy?

I sat facing west, the early afternoon sun reflecting brightly off the snow covered lake. I slipped my sunglasses on. It would be another month at least before the ice would melt completely but no one cared; "Let's just get outside and enjoy the sunshine," was the rallying cry of the day, and people jumped to it.

Overhead planes staged in a ragged line one by one, readying themselves for their final approach to Minneapolis's huge international airport. It was five miles behind me to the east, and big tri-engine jets seemed to float through the air as they began their decent, one after another, lowering themselves out of the sky, loud engines roaring through the peaceful afternoon.

Unlike most people, I am not bothered by airplane noise. I'm predisposed to like them because my dad had been a pilot. His only job his entire life was flying airplanes. He'd been a young pilot in the Navy in World War II and then flown for a major airline right up until the day he died at his home in Seattle at the relatively young age of forty-seven. "Heart attack," is what they said at the time. I always wondered if it had something to do with a little early morning fooling around with the woman he'd been married to at the time, a young lady only seven years older than me.

But that was a long time ago; a lifetime really, so why was it that thoughts of him were flooding back to me now on this sunniest of days in the middle of March? I was fifteen when he'd left, my two brothers much younger. Mom was only forty-two, but my memories today, though clouded by time and probably romanticized a bit, were not to be denied: Dad coaching my little league baseball team, Dad putting up football goal posts in the backyard for me to practice place kicking, Dad showing home movies of our family on vacation in Montana, Dad teaching me how to care for a car, Dad talking to me about how to act around girls. Dad being a dad.

But he left when I was fifteen, there was no doubt about that. He left and I never saw much of him after that. Eight years later he died.

Died, but didn't. He's still been with me, that smiling face of his, carried in my heart all these years. I was down at this same lake a few weeks after I'd heard of his passing. It was a burning hot summer in mid-July. I had been out for a bike ride and was not having much luck shaking the lost feeling I had because of his untimely death, knowing I'd never see him again. I had stopped at a bench much like the one I was on now and was looking out over the sparkling water, gazing at nothing really, thoughts turned inward. Suddenly, above the lake a vision caught my eye; a vision of a plane soaring through the sky, a cross between a jet and a passenger plane. I watched as Dad opened the cockpit window, dressed in his best dark blue captain's uniform, looking natty. He waved and smiled and waved some more.

27

I was filled with such a sense of peace, then, seeing him, that I nearly cried with joy. Well, truth be told, I did. I cried and then wiped the tears from my eyes and happily waved back. He might have passed from this world, but he was going to be all right; he was still flying the planes he loved to fly. He was going to be okay.

Maybe that's what was happening now, on this sunny late winter day by the lake. Maybe each and every one of those planes flying by overhead was Dad's way of saying, "Hi, there son. Good to see you."

Sounds weird? Maybe, but I took it for what it was, Dad and I communicating with each other in our own way after all these years. And with that realization, poof, my melancholy mood vanished. It was good to have him with me.

I pulled myself back to the present and went back to watching the parade of folks strolling by, everyone enjoying the sunshine and the warmth of a mild winter's day. Overhead, plane after plane after plane continued to pass, each one of them like so many memories of my dad still alive and carried inside me.

Suddenly, there was a petulant tap on my shoulder.

"Hey, Dad. What are you doing? Mom's worried."

I turned. It was my oldest son. I had been thinking about going to visit him before I'd been derailed by a beckoning park bench and a plunge into all those remembrances of my father. "Hey there Jeremy. Good to see you." I smiled at him.

My six year old grandson Shawn ran up and gave me a big hug. "Hi Grandpa. Look at these." He pointed out his new rubber boots that were already spattered with mud. From what I could tell they had a spider man pattern on them.

"Those look pretty sharp, young man."

28

Shawn grinned and hurried off to a nearby slush puddle where he began an enthusiastic game of simply stomping around in it.

Jeremy walked around the bench. He was tall and he hovered over me, blocking the sun. He asked again, his tone pinched and barely patient, "Dad what are you doing? Mom's worried. She called me to check on you. She thought you might be down here. You didn't answer your phone. You have it turned off?"

"I don't think so." I took my phone from my pocket and checked it. Oops. Damn. He was right, I'd inadvertently turned it off. "Hey, I'm sorry. I screwed up."

Jeremy sighed, took out his phone and made a call. He and I had a close relationship. He lived in the city, not far from both the lake and his sister. We talked regularly and I saw Shawn and his older sister Emily at least once a week, when I drove in from where Elise and I lived twenty miles away in Orchard Lake to take care of them after school.

I said, "I was just enjoying the sun and thinking about things. What are you guys up to?"

Jeremy held up a hand. "Yeah, Mom, I found him. He's fine. Okay. Yeah. Is it okay if we pick you up in a little while?" He turned to me and grinned. "Yeah, Mom, I'll tell him. Okay. I think maybe we'll go for a walk. I got Shawn some new boots. It's a nice day out. Dad's good. Okay. I'll tell him. Bye."

Jeremy hung up, bent down, looked me in the eye and said, "Mom says to call her next time you decide to wander off all afternoon. If you don't there'll be hell to pay."

I smiled. I knew Elise wasn't really too mad, just concerned, and she was right. I'd messed up, no excuses. "I promise I'll call next time," I told Jeremy.

"Good. Now," he grinned and clapped his hands

enthusiastically together, "how about if we all go for a little stroll and enjoy this wonderful day?"

I wouldn't have passed up a chance to spend time like this with my son and grandson for the world.

I stood up. "I'm all for it. Let's go."

Shawn ran over and took me by the hand and we all started for the path around the lake.

As we walked, Jeremy clasped me on my shoulder and smiled. "Good to see you, Dad."

I grinned back at him and spontaneously gave him a tight hug. "Good to see you, too, son."

We started walking along the path, Shawn running ahead, laughing. It was great to be with my family. I was a lucky man.

A minute later, while Jeremy and Shawn were preoccupied throwing snowballs at the trunk of a large oak tree, I turned and waved at a low flying passenger plane. Then I joined them in their game. I hadn't bothered to tell Jeremy that his grandfather would be joining us on our walk. Not today anyway. For now, it'd be my little secret. Just between Dad and me.

Sweeping Out the Garage

The old man spent more than a few minutes at his task, taking his time as if there was nothing more important to do on this cloudy December day than sweep out the garage. He used a push broom; a long wooden pole with worn, bent, black bristles that he pulled towards himself instead of pushing, making you wonder why he did it that way.

He'd tell you that pulling did a better job, at least in his estimation, and he was methodical in his task, starting at the far right hand corner and working his way across the two car space to the left, getting up piles of sand and gravel and grit, all accumulated during the last few weeks of rain, then snow, then rain. There was a lot of debris and he was sweeping the cracked concrete surface with a deliberation that after a while made you begin to admire him for being so conscientious.

Above him in the rafters a red squirrel had taken up residence, scattering chewed up bits of black walnut hulls and pulverized shell powder all over the place, adding to the mess not only on the floor, but his workbench as well.

"What a nuisance," the old man muttered, scratching his beard and adjusting the stocking hat his wife had knitted for him before she died. "Damn thing acts like it owns the place."

He unscrewed the brush part of the broom from the handle and used it to sweep the surface which was positioned directly below where a majority of hulls had been stored; hulls that, as he swept, came tumbling onto the floor bouncing and rolling with an entropy all of their own.

Watching them scatter, he sighed, thinking, *I should probably do something about that damn squirrel.* It was a thought he had every year, coming up with the same answer every time. *Maybe next year.*

He didn't notice, but up in the rafters the red squirrel was watching. Normally a loud, aggressive species, it was content to look down and keep an eye on the old man, soon becoming hypnotized by the way he worked, back and forth, sweeping and sweeping. After a while its eyes grew weary, then heavy. Then, too heavy to watch anymore, the mesmerized squirrel fell into a deep sleep, dreaming of the thousands of black walnuts stored in the safety of the rafters, with an entire winter ahead and all the time in the world to crack them open.

The squirrel could have no way of knowing, of course, but it had been like that for a few years, the old man's obsession with cleaning out the garage. Ever since he'd lost his dear wife to cancer two and a half years earlier he'd felt compelled to keep things clean; both inside the home they'd shared for over forty years and outside.

To be honest, she had been the one to do the inside work and he the outside during their married life; a silently agreed upon division of labour. It had served them well. But with her gone he had taken it upon himself to do both. He'd never measure up to her standards when it came to cleaning and dusting of course, but he tried. He did his best. He was pretty sure she'd be pleased.

But it was the outside work, like taking care of the gardens or cutting the grass or for sure sweeping out the garage, that made him feel in his element. He did it with a care and a passion that, if you took the time to watch and think about, was really quite remarkable.

Remarkable maybe or, at the very least, touching; this old man, living by himself, sweeping out the garage on a mild winter's day. Watched over by a sleepy red squirrel as he moved across the floor, sweeping and cleaning, all the while remembering the past and all those good years he and his wife spent together. Those good years and their life long bond and how they had enjoyed working together and taking care of their home, both inside and out.

When he was finished he put the broom away and closed the garage door. The squirrel awoke, scrounged a nut and began eating, scattering shell pieces to the floor.

Snow flurries were in the air as the old man slowly shuffled towards the back door, glad that for a short time at least the garage floor was clean. He adjusted his hat and smiled, thinking of his wife. He had done his part and a good job. He was sure she'd be happy.

Hunting Crows

Dad pointed. "Tyler, take this bag and put those decoys way out by the corn stalks. Not too close to us. We don't want to spook them."

I dutifully followed his instructions and hiked through the snow, my breath steaming in the twenty degree air. I put out about a dozen black, bird-like shapes in the middle of the huge field like he'd asked, then hurried back to where we were setting up our position, just over a small rise, two-hundred feet away.

"That look okay?"

Dad made a big deal of looking at them through his binoculars. "No, damn it. They're too close together. Go spread them out. Hurry, the crows could be here any minute."

I worked my way across the corn field reduced to stubble by last month's fall tilling and moved them further apart, then jogged back, panting a little. I was in pretty good shape from playing basketball in school, but the snow was over a foot deep and hard to move in.

I plopped down on the canvas tarp Dad had set out. "Okay, now?"

He took a quick look. "Yeah, they're fine," he mumbled, like he'd already lost interest. Then he removed his whiskey flask from his jacket pocket, took a drink, and set about getting his gun ready.

Killing crows. Not my idea of a good time. I had nothing against them or any other living creature for that matter. What a rotten way to spend the day, but I was with my old man so I guess that counted for something.

Dad and Mom divorced last summer. My guess was that Dad's drinking had something to do with it, although his inability to keep a job may have contributed. Mom started hanging around with Jerry Kowalski and one thing had led to another.

My girlfriend Trish said that Dad deserved it. "He was kind of a jerk to her, Ty. I don't blame her for kicking him out."

Which might have been true, but I missed having Dad at home. I was fifteen and my two younger sisters and I saw him one night a week and every other weekend. Jerry Kowalski was nice enough, but who knew how long he'd stick around? He didn't drink like Dad, but the man liked his weed, that was for sure. He even offered some to me once, which I turned down. Trish says I should tell my mom. I'm thinking about it, but I really don't want to cause a scene, so... I don't know. We'll see.

Anyway, Dad figured taking me hunting with him would be a good way for us to spend what they call Quality Time together. I'd have been happy enough playing Fortnite on the X-Box with him like we normally did, but what the hell.

"At least you'll be getting some fresh air," he tried to joke earlier that morning as we got ready. "Just dress for it. Put on some extra thick long underwear or something. You'll be fine."

Yeah, right. Now here I was lying on a tarp in the middle of a field with it freezing cold outside and the sky a depressing grey. My toes inside my boots were already numb. Fun times.

While he got his gun ready I did the same with mine. It was a bolt action twenty-two with long rifle bullets and a six shell clip. His words came back to me, 'Remember to hold the rifle steady and line up the bead on the end of the barrel with the sight. When the crow's body fills the sight, slowly squeeze the trigger.'

We'd practiced that fall on Dad's friend's land, the land we were on now, a few miles outside of town and a mile from the trailer park where Mom and I and my two sisters lived along with Jerry. I was as ready as I'd ever be.

We lay on the tarp for about half an hour before the crows came. Dad sipped from his flask while I tried to pretend I wasn't freezing to death. Strangely enough, though, the longer I was outside the more I began to enjoy being in the wide open spaces. Maybe I was just one-hundred percent numb from the cold and couldn't think straight, but I have to admit that it wasn't too bad being out in nature. I even saw a fox run along the edge of the woods and an eagle soaring over the field. It was pretty cool.

We heard their "Caw, caw, cawing" way before we saw them. Then they came in over the trees on the far side of the field, a big flock of maybe thirty crows that all landed next to the decoys I'd set out. I took a prideful moment to congratulate myself on doing such a good job, but Dad couldn't be bothered to thank me. Instead, he took a long drink from his flask and picked up his gun. "Okay," he whispered. "This is it. Get your rifle ready."

I took the safety off, lay the gun on the top of the rise and sighted. It took a few seconds before I had one dead on. Then I moved the barrel a little. I knew exactly what I was going to do.

"Ready?" Dad whispered.

"Yeah."

"Okay. We'll shoot together on the count of three. One... Two..."

On the count of "two" I aimed thirty feet in front of the crow and pulled the trigger. The rifle barked a loud bang, followed by a puff of snow out in the field. The crows immediately took off, just as Dad fired a moment after me on the count of "three". He missed everything.

"What the hell?" He jumped to his feet and yelled, towering over me, "What'd you do that for?"

36

I left my rifle on the tarp and stood up to face him. He was a head taller than me and seventy pounds heavier, but he needed to know. "Dad, I'm not going to kill a crow just to make you happy."

I thought he might hit me right then and there but he didn't. Instead, he grabbed me by my jacket and shook me. Hard. I stumbled backwards, but kept my balance. He got right in my face and yelled, "What are you, anyway? Some kind of pansy? We Lathrup's have always hunted. We've never had a problem killing things. What's wrong with you?"

I was scared. I'd never stood up to him before, but all the anger I felt towards him leaving my mom and sisters and me spilled over into a red rage. I swear to God I almost slugged him but I didn't. Instead, I kept my voice measured and calm and said, "I'm not going to kill a defenceless creature just to please you."

The old man pushed me away and said menacingly, "To hell with you, then."

I'd had it with him. I walked away with no idea where I was going, but I did know this – it was time I started sticking up for myself. Behind me, I heard him yelling for me to get back there or there'd be hell to pay.

Too bad, I thought to myself, as I started running. The old man would have to catch me first. I felt liberated and happy. Like I could run forever. I just might.

Leatherwork

Ernie Schaefer undid the twine and rolled the stiff leather onto his worktable, smoothing it out. His practiced eyes scanned the surface noting some prominent stretch marks, deciding at that very moment to incorporate them into the project he was starting. Before he began, however, he took a moment to think about the cow whose hide he now had in front of him. The animal had once been alive, and if it hadn't spent its time strolling imaginary fields munching on sweet, fragrant clover, at least it had once been a living breathing creature of the earth. He felt in his heart a reverence for the animal and he bent his head for a moment in a silent prayer of thanks. Then he began to work.

He was a retired shoe repair man, or cobbler, as he sometimes let slip if the moment was right. Working with leather was in his blood and he'd been doing it all his life; which might be considered odd, since he grew up in the city, far from any farms or ranches or small towns that may have fostered his craft, but that's the way it was.

Ernie was first exposed to leather crafting in junior high shop class back in the late fifties. His first project had been a hand-tooled bookmark and by the time he had finished he was hooked. His parents, sensing his enthusiasm, bought him a Tandy Leather Making Kit for Christmas that year. His fate was sealed by the tools of the trade: a swivel knife for carving, stamping tools for creating intricate designs and a multiuse rawhide mallet.

In high school, while others got jobs at restaurants or gas stations, Ernie found work at a Xavier's Shoe Repair in downtown Minneapolis. Xavier Dukakas was a second generation immigrant from Greece. He was a robust man, short in stature and long in enthusiasm, who took a liking to the skinny kid who happened to love working with leather as much as he did. Ernie called him Mr. Dukakas and the patient man taught his young protégé everything he knew about the craft of shoe repair.

"You hold the shoe firmly but gently," he told Ernie more than once when he was learning to finish the edge of a re-soled shoe on the burnishing wheel. "Like an egg," he said, pantomiming massaging one in his hands. Then he laughed. "Or your girlfriend," he added grinning, watching the young man's ears turn red.

Ernie eventually got the knack, learning from the older man that most things worth doing well in life required practice, and practice required patience. In truth, Mr. Dukakas was much more than an employer; he was a mentor, and Ernie worked for him until old age forced his retirement. Mr. Dukakas sold the business to him for a fair price and Ernie continued to run it until he retired at the age of sixty-nine. He then sold the shop to an industrious young couple who wanted to use the space to start their own micro-brewery.

Life went on.

A few years after he retired, Ernie was outside working in the garden that he and his wife Nora maintained with loving care. He was just transplanting some hosta when she came up to him carrying a worn box, split at the sides and held together with masking tape.

"Look what I came across in the storage room. Your old leather kit."

Ernie stiffly got to his feet and wiped his hands on his overalls. She handed it to him and he held it reverently. "I haven't seen this in years."

"You know you could set up a work space downstairs in the furnace room," she said. "You always enjoyed doing your leatherwork."

The moment he took the lid off the box memories came

flooding back: the projects he'd made, the aroma of the leather, the smell of the dye and feel of the hide. He smiled at Nora, not needing to be persuaded further. "Good idea."

Ernie has had his workshop now for five years. He has a website where he sells his 'Creations' as he calls them: purses, journal covers and cases. He gladly accepts orders, like the one he is working on today, a case for an iPhone 6s. He takes a tag board template he has made and uses an awl to mark out an outline on the leather. He uses a razor blade knife to cut out the pattern. Then he trims the edges with a skiving tool and punches out holes so he can eventually put the case together. Today's work ends with him dying the leather deep violet, the colour the customer requested. Tomorrow he will apply Neatsfoot Oil and the following day he will finish it with Carnauba Cream and hand-stitch the case together with durable waxed thread. Then he will ship it to the customer. He loves the steps in the process and he loves working with his hands. He loves the feel of the leather. He loves the aroma in his workshop. He loves it all.

He is setting the piece aside to dry when the back door upstairs opens. He hears a familiar voice talking to Nora and smiles. Then there are footsteps hurrying down the steps and he turns to greet his grandson.

"Charlie," he says, eyes bright with affection, "how's my boy?" Charlie is eleven years old and has been helping Ernie for over a year, showing the same love of leather Ernie had at that age; a fact he still considers amazing given that in an age of electronics there is this kid who likes to work with his hands.

"I'm good, Grandpa," Charlie says, and then spies the cell phone case. "New project?"

"Yep, it came in today." Ernie can't help but notice the disappointment on the boy's face.

"Oh...I wish I could have helped."

"You can," Ernie grins and watches as Charlie's eyes light up. "You definitely can. The order was for two."

"That's great," his grandson says happily.

Ernie tells him, "In fact, I've been thinking about something. You've helped me long enough. I think now it's time for you to make this one on your own."

Their eyes meet, each of them knowing that something special has taken place, something just between the two of them. They don't have to say anything.

Then Charlie's expression turns serious. He carefully selects a piece of leather and lays it out on the worktable. He runs his hands over the hide and closes his eyes and is quiet for a few moments.

When he is ready he looks at his grandpa and smiles. Then he begins to work.

Sugarfoot

Colby Stackhouse crested the top of the hill in the stolen car and knew right away he was in trouble. The cop car up ahead was pointed right at him fifty yards away on the other side of the interstate. Colby was doing ninety-five miles an hour as he flew past. The cop hit the flashers, pulled a U-turn, bumped across the grassy median and came after him, tires burning rubber. Colby had about one second to decide if he was going to make a run for it or not. He decided to go for it and stomped on the gas. There was no way he was going back to prison.

Young Farley Shiffler, a three year officer with the North Dakota Highway Patrol, was settling in on Colby's tail and was about to radio headquarters when his rear tire blew and he had to pull over to the side of the interstate, watching Colby and the stolen black Honda disappear over the next rise.

"Geez it, man," he said under his breath, which was about as close to swearing as Farley ever got. He was mad as a bucket of rattlesnakes and, again, nearly cursed his bad luck. "Shoot," he muttered, slamming his fist on the steering wheel of his squad car.

Embarrassed, he called in and reported to his superior. "We've got a problem," he said when Captain Shane Hutchinson came on the radio and Farley filled him in on what had taken place.

The Captain didn't hold back in dressing down his young highway patrolman, liberally using words that made Farley's ears turn red. When he was done and starting to calm down, Hutchinson told Farley to get the tire fixed and he'd send Steven Lightfoot out to meet him at the next exit.

"We've got to find this guy," Hutchinson said. "He stole that poor bastard's car this morning, right down the road from where he got let out of prison in Bismarck. He'd

42

been there eleven years for manufacturing drugs. You'd think he'd learned a lesson, but apparently not. He's an idiot and dangerous to boot. We've got to get him."

"Yes, sir."

Farley signed off, fixed his tire and drove two miles west to the Beach Springs Wayside Rest, where he met up with his fellow officer, Steven Lightfoot, a veteran of twenty one years with the highway patrol.

Lightfoot walked over when the squad car pulled up. "Hey there, Farley," he said with a tight smile. "Rough day, huh?" It was just after nine in the morning.

"You can say that again." Farley got out of his car and filled Lightfoot in on what had happened.

When he was done, all Lightfoot said was, "Hey, don't beat yourself up over it, man. It could happen to anyone."

Farley liked Lightfoot a lot and the feeling was mutual. A three-quarter blood Cree whose ancestors were from Alberta, Lightfoot had taken a shine to Farley from day one on the force, taking time to show him how to be a good, conscientious patrolman.

Farley was a quiet but attentive student, which probably helped because Lightfoot was a man of few words. He and Farley could spend hours together with only a minimum of conversation between them.

As Farley told his wife Lesley once, "I figure if I talk too much, Lightfoot will just ignore me."

Lesley laughed at the time and said, "Well, just shut up, then. Watch and listen and learn."

Which is what Farley did.

He was running the options of what they should do next through his mind when Lightfoot said, "I told Hutchinson we should probably call in Benson. You know how the Captain gets, the guy is such a cheap mother, but if we can catch this Colby, it'll make him look good."

"Is he bringing Sugarfoot?"

"Yeah." Lightfoot checked his watch. "Should be here in half an hour." He paused and looked around. Let's go sit over there."

Farley and Lightfoot went over to a picnic table set up by a pair of beat up trash cans. The shade was provided by a covered structure that was bare wood, the paint having been sand blasted off by the relentless North Dakota wind.

"You know that wayside rest on the border?" Lightfoot asked, cupping a hand rolled cigarette and lighting it with a stick match. "McKenzie Unit?"

Farley nodded. "Yeah."

"There was a patrol car there. Larry Winston. He never saw our guy Colby." Lightfoot looked to the west, smoking. "It's twelve miles to the border. Our guy probably turned off somewhere between here and there."

"I'll go get my map." Farley jogged to the car, grabbed his county map and came back, spreading it on the picnic table and holding it down as best he could, silently cursing, *Flippin' wind.*

Lightfoot picked up a few rocks to weigh down the map and contemplated it for a moment. "Look, here's where we are, and here's where Wilson is." Farley peered over Lightfoot's shoulder. The county map showed the area in great detail. "There's only a couple of roads our guy could have turned off on." Lightfoot pointed and Farley looked closely. "Two to the north and one to the south." He looked some more, thinking. "North goes up to the Badlands, south goes out onto the prairies. All three of those roads eventually peter out." He snubbed out his cigarette, crushing it under his boot heel. "No matter which direction he went, that's rough country out there. It's a good thing Benson and Sugarfoot will be with us."

Just then a battered pickup pulled into the parking area,

dust billowing up around it. It came to a stop near where the squad cars were parked. The driver's door opened and out stepped Benson Beaudein who tipped his sweat stained cowboy hat and said, "Hey cousin, looks like you need some help." He smiled, his long dark hair blowing around his face. "You figured out a plan yet, or do you want me to do it for you?"

Lightfoot laughed. "Good to see you, too, cousin. Come over here and sit down. Bring Sugarfoot. I haven't seen that old boy in a while."

Sugarfoot was a dark tawny-coloured bloodhound named for the white foot on the paw of his back left leg. He had helped out in searches before and was considered better than any human being when it came to tracking. Earlier that spring he and Benson had been called in on a Search and Rescue mission up north in the Theodore Roosevelt Badlands. A young couple with their five year old daughter had been camping and when they awoke in the morning the child was missing. The girl's father had immediately let the park rangers know what had happened and help had been called in. After searching throughout the morning with no results a park ranger suggested they call in Benson and Sugarfoot.

When they arrived the affable bloodhound was shown the little girl's favourite doll. Taking a moment to absorb the scent he put his nose to the ground and headed out into the rugged, unforgiving country of the badlands.

It took about two hours, but eventually they found her safe and unharmed wedged behind a boulder. Benson gave the little girl her doll and comforted her while getting her to drink some water. She told him she'd climbed behind the boulder trying to stay warm during the night and when she'd awoken in the morning she'd been too scared to move. All the while she told her story she kept a tight hold on her doll. But she also kept hugging Sugarfoot who soaked up the attention, tongue lolling and eyes rolling, panting happily and clearly appreciating the little girl's attention.

Now a few months later both Lightfoot and Farley knew that with Benson with them, Sugarfoot was the key to tracking down Colby.

All three of them went over the map again, Lightfoot and Farley taking occasional moments to scratch Sugarfoot's big head and talk to him. Both patrolmen had a fond affection for the bloodhound.

Benson lived on a small ranch on the north side of Interstate 94, about ten miles from where they were now. It was entirely possible that Colby could be headed in that direction.

"But I kind of doubt it," Benson said, when they talked about it. "That's bad country out there. Hard to get around unless you know what you're doing, which doesn't sound like our guy." He wiped sweat off his face. "Warm today." He patted Sugarfoot. "I'll have to keep this old boy hydrated." Then he looked at the map some more. Like Lightfoot, Benson usually didn't tend to elaborate too much.

Farley sat quietly, observing the interaction between the two cousins. Benson wore jeans, cowboy boots and a blue and white checked snap button shirt. On his left wrist he had on a tooled silver and turquoise bracelet. His sun worn face was lined and his teeth were a brilliant white when he smiled, which wasn't often.

Benson and Lightfoot got along well, Farley could tell. He knew that Benson had a wife, Charlotte, but they didn't have any children. Benson and Lightfoot were nearly the same age, late forties, and they were both around five feet ten inches tall, with lean, muscular builds. Lightfoot wore his hair short. Other than that, they could be mistaken for twins.

A call came in to Lightfoot's radio and he ran over to his squad car. He listened for a few minutes, turning serious. He signed off and came back. "Good and bad news, boys. First, the good news. A rancher called in reporting a black Honda heading south down County Road Forty Four. Said it almost hit one of his longhorns."

"The Little Missouri Trail?" Farley asked.

"Yep. He's heading for the river."

"What's the bad news?"

"He's got a gun," Lightfoot answered, frowning. "The guy he stole it from told the Dickenson police that he had his rifle in the trunk. Used it for deer and antelope hunting. A 30-06 with a box of twenty five shells."

"Dang," Farley said, to which Lightfoot smiled. He kind of got a kick out of the kid.

Benson was unfazed. He stood up and said, "Well, let's go get him." He scratched Sugarfoot behind the ears. "You all ready, boy?"

Sugarfoot looked up at his owner with what looked like love or at least affection in his eyes. Farley could have sworn he saw the dog blink, *Yes*.

Farley went with Lightfoot in his squad car and Benson followed in his pickup with Sugarfoot. County Road Forty Four also known as The Little Missouri River Trail was down the interstate about five miles. They were there in four minutes. They turned left and followed the road to the south, speeding by the turn off where the rancher lived that called in the Honda sighting. The blacktop pavement then gave way to gravel, and then to sand, and then it just ended.

They stopped and got out, looking around. The prairie lay out ahead of them, rolling grassland and sage stretching all the way to the horizon. But it was deceptive because there were also gullies and ridges carved out by the constant wind and the meagre amount of rain that fell in the region. On the horizon to the west and south was Sentinel Butte, at 3,400 feet the highest point of land around. They could also see the meandering outline of cottonwood trees which showed the course of the Little Missouri River. They could also see tire tracks heading off in the distance.

Lightfoot wanted to be cautious and get the lie of the land. "Let's go on foot from here."

Benson had brought supplies in three day packs containing food and water. They each shouldered one, taking a moment to drink.

"We don't want to get dehydrated," Benson said, pouring some water into a bowl for Sugarfoot. "Especially, this old boy." His patted his dog. "A bloodhound like him needs to keep his fluids up. I'll also keep his nose moist. It helps him search out the scent better, especially when it's warm like this."

The other men nodded. It was early summer, not a cloud in the sky and the temperature was expected get into the eighties later that afternoon. Hot weather was not the best weather for tracking but they didn't have much choice. They'd have to do their best.

After they'd drunk their fill they started off walking in the direction of the tire tracks figuring they were Colby's. They were. A quarter mile ahead on the other side of a low ridge they saw the Honda mired in sand at the bottom of a shallow depression in the land. It looked abandoned. They cautiously approached, Lightfoot and Farley with their revolvers drawn, but the car was empty. Lightfoot motioned that it was okay for Benson to approach.

"Not the best car for out here," Lightfoot pointed out.

Benson came up with Sugarfoot on his leash and showed him the Honda. The bloodhound sniffed around inside the car and then outside. He put his head up into the wind, sniffing some more. Lightfoot wet a bandana and applied it to Sugarfoot's nose and gave him some water to drink. Then, after making a few false moves he put his head to the ground heading west and south toward the Little Missouri River pulling Benson along, Lightfoot and Farley following close behind.

The three men were all experienced when it came to being out on the plains, Farley because of his young age only slightly less so than Lightfoot and Benson. He had the brief image in his mind of Sherlock Holms. *The game is afoot.* But he shook his head to get rid of it as he holstered his revolver. He needed to focus. He checked his watch. It read 10:47 am. It had been nearly two hours since he'd last seen Colby. He jogged to catch up to Lightfoot and Benson who were following Sugarfoot across the rolling grassland plains.

The area of North Dakota they were searching was part of the Dakota National Grasslands which comprised over a million acres in the western portion of the state. Within the boundaries were portions of state-owned and privately owned land, much of it leased by cattle ranchers for grazing. Out where they were, there were no buildings or indications of any ranches. Wide open spaces was the term that came to Farley's mind.

After about fifteen minutes of hiking they reached another rise. From there the land rolled downhill for about five miles to the Little Missouri River. Benson took out a pair of binoculars and scanned to the south and west. The rolling grasslands belied the fact that there were gullies, ravines and low ridges throughout the area. Colby could be hiding anywhere.

"If he makes it to the river it'll be almost impossible to find him," Benson said, pulling his cowboy hat tight and squinting into the sun. "I don't see any movement out on the hills."

"Let's turn Sugarfoot loose, then," Lightfoot said.

Benson shook his head in the negative. "I'm going to keep him on the leash. It'll be safer than all of us than running around like a herd of antelope. We'll just take it slow and easy." He looked through the binoculars again, thinking. Then he added, "Don't worry. We'll get him."

They started off walking, Benson keeping a firm hand on Sugarfoot, who was straining on the lease and clearly on the trail. Lightfoot and Farley followed behind. Colby was out there somewhere. Farley hoped Benson was right. Hoped they'd get him soon. If they didn't get him by nightfall...Well, he didn't want to think about it. Colby had that rifle. It put a whole different spin on things.

Colby was out there all right and figuring that by now the authorities were out to get him. When he'd jammed the car into the sand and gotten stuck he'd cursed his luck before getting out, yelling and kicking the front tire until his big toe started hurting.

Finally he stopped and took stock of his situation. He had the rifle he'd found in the trunk when he'd made a pit stop in Dickenson. He had half a bag of Doritos and a nearly full quart bottle of coke he'd bought at a Quik Stop outside of Medora. That was about it. The prison had given him the clothes he was now wearing: a pair of running shoes, socks, blue jeans, long sleeve work shirt, white under shirt, jean jacket and a green John Deer baseball hat.

While in prison he had bulked up to a muscular two hundred and twenty pounds and felt he was in pretty good shape. He looked to the west and south. *God, what desolate country*. He saw a line of trees that he assumed ran along the banks of a river out near the horizon. He rolled up his jean jacket and put it along with the chips, pop and box of rifle shells in the plastic bag from the Quik Stop. He kept six shells out of the box to load the rifle and then hung it over his right shoulder with its strap. All set.

He took off toward the river at a slow jog, until a few minutes later when he tripped over a partially hidden rock and fell. He ripped a hole in his jeans where his knee came up against the hard ground. It hurt and was bleeding. Cursing to himself, he got up, dabbed at the blood and collected his things, walking this time, forcing himself to slow down as he carefully made his way across the grasslands.

In less than a quarter of a mile he found a gully and climbed down into it. It seemed to slope towards the river in the distance. The going was slower, but he felt okay about that. He was being safe and keeping out of sight, using the sun to direct him. He'd grown up in this country and knew as much about taking care of himself as the next person. At least that's what he kept telling himself as the sun rose higher and higher and the day kept getting warmer and warmer. He pushed on, not wanting to get caught.

Sugarfoot found the spot on the ground with Colby's blood on it. The men gathered around while Benson examined it. Standing up he said, "It looks like our guy was running and fell." Benson shook his head. "Not the smartest thing to do."

"I don't think our guy's all that sharp," Lightfoot commented. "Not the brightest bulb in the pack." Looking out over the sloping grasslands, he muttered, "Wonder where he is?"

Benson took a break to give Sugarfoot some water and wet his nose. Then he knelt down and looked the dog in its eyes. "Let's go find him, big fella."

Again, the dog seemed to understand perfectly what Benson was saying. He gave a quiet woof and turned in the direction Colby was traveling, nose to the ground. "Let's go," Benson said, motioning for Lightfoot and Farley to follow. "Our escapee might be moving a little slower now."

A quarter mile ahead they came to the gully that Colby had dropped into. They stopped and contemplated their next move. Lightfoot and Benson were talking with their heads bent together. Farley just listened, keeping his mouth shut and paying attention. He was just fine being the third place guy on this trip. He could learn a lot from Lightfoot and Benson.

They decided that Benson and Sugarfoot would go into the gully to make sure they were on the right trail and that Colby didn't climb out at some point. Lightfoot and Farley would follow up above along the edge. That way they could watch the land out ahead of them for any movement.

Before they started off, though, they took a break and had some more water. Benson suggested they each have a granola bar from their pack. "Got to keep our energy up," he said, ripping open the wrapper. He also pulled out a Tupperware container with dry dog food and gave Sugarfoot a handful. He gave him some more water, too. The three men sat on their heels, resting, drinking from their water bottles. Farley checked his watch. It was just about noon.

"Getting warmer and warmer," he commented. Benson nodded.

"Yeah, it is," Lightfoot said and then was quiet looking out over the land, adjusting the brim of his hat. A man of few words. After a few minutes, he stood up. "Let's get going." He looked at Benson. "You ready?"

"Yep." He wet Sugarfoot's nose and gave him a tug on his leash. The dog stood up, ready to go. "Let's do it."

Benson and Sugarfoot dropped into the gully and started down it, Lightfoot and Farley following up above. It was slow going for Benson and his bloodhound. There were piles of rocks scattered along the ground that they had to step over or around.

Up where Lightfoot and Farley walked, the prairie continued slopping towards the river. The land was dry and mixed with sagebrush and prairie grasses that crunched under their boots. Farley noticed Little Blue Stem and Indian Grass growing among the rock and gravel. There weren't a lot of areas of prairie left anymore in this part of the country, or anywhere else for that matter, and he was happy to see a few native grasses alive and thriving. It made him feel good, connected to the land.

Every now and then Farley caught a glimpse of Benson and Sugarfoot working their way through the gully below them.

"I'm glad we've got those two with us," he said, pointing.

"Me, too."

"They seem good with each other."

"Yeah, they are." Lightfoot kept walking, but glanced over and added, "They're different, though, Benson and Sugarfoot. They're tied to each other somehow. They both care about each other, that's plain to see, but they also care about who they're looking for. A lot."

"Even about someone like Colby?" Farley asked.

"Yeah, even about someone like him," Lightfoot said. "To those two it's all the same. Someone is out there and probably needs help, so that's what they are trying to do." Lightfoot looked around as he walked, sweat beading up on his face. "It's what keeps them going. The chance to help even someone like Colby out."

Farley wasn't sure if he got all of it or not, but he was

glad that they had Benson and Sugarfoot with them. They'd never had been able to track Colby through the rugged land on their own.

The next few hours their search party slowly and carefully made their way toward the Little Missouri. "We've got to keep a lookout for this guy," Lightfoot kept saying. "He could be out here, anywhere. I don't like that he has that 30-06."

Farley nodded in agreement and kept his eyes constantly moving, scanning for any movement ahead of them. But all was quiet. The only things moving were the waves of heat rising off the scorched, baking prairie and the windblown dust, swirling across the land.

The gully eventually came to an end into a dry wash riverbed that followed the natural landscape to the right. Who knew how many centuries it had been there? Sugarfoot wanted to keep following and stay on the scent trail, but Benson had other ideas and climbed out of the gully helping Sugarfoot scramble up the steep incline.

"Let's take a breather," he said, reaching the top.

They were only a few miles from the Little Missouri. He took his pack off and poured out some water and set the bowl down, which Sugarfoot eagerly lapped up.

"Do you think we'll ever get him?" Farley asked, trying not to sound discouraged.

Lightfoot nodded. "Yeah, we'll get him." He indicated towards Benson. "What do you think?"

"No doubt in my mind," Benson said, looking with affection at his dog. "This old boy still has a lot of get up and go in him, don't you, fella?"

He was reaching over to scratch Sugarfoot's ears when all of a sudden a shot ran out. Instantly they flattened themselves to the ground, Benson pulling Sugarfoot up close to him. Farley had his face in the dirt, the sand hot on his cheek. He was shaking with an adrenaline rush mixture of fear and excitement.

Benson cautioned, "Everyone let's keep calm." Probably as much for Farley's sake as anyone else's.

After about a minute, Lightfoot raised his head and peered in the direction of the shot. It had come from where they figured Colby was heading. He looked at Benson. "Give me those binoculars." After scanning the plains for a few minutes he said, "I don't see anything."

"What do think that was all about?" Farley asked. "Do you think he was shooting at us?"

"I don't know," Lightfoot said, and turned to Benson. "What do you think?"

Benson considered the question for a few seconds and then shrugged his shoulders. "You've got me. I have no idea."

They lay flat on the ground for a few more minutes, Lightfoot scanning the countryside. Finally he declared that the coast was clear. Standing up, he said, "Let's head down that way." He pointed to the dry river bed. It ran in the direction where the shot had come from. "Find out what the heck's going on."

What was going on, was that Colby had run into a prairie rattlesnake and lost a short, but decisive battle.

When the gully he'd been following ended, Colby decided to follow the dry, sandy riverbed as it curved to the right. Over the centuries it had cut a path through the rock and gravel so that the banks were now nearly fifteen feet high. Colby walked along the sandy river bottom feeling safe and hidden from sight. By now he figured that someone would be following him. After all, that cop had tried to chase him back on the interstate. It was only a matter of time before they'd send a search party out looking

55

for him. Colby had no plan. Instead he followed his instincts, and these told him to stay in the river bed, so that's what he did.

He soon found that it meandered in a serpentine manner following the contour of the land, and heading, Colby guessed, towards the river. The sun baked off the dry sand, turning the river bed into an oven. Colby had long since choked down the last of the chips as well as the hot coke. Not a pleasant meal by any stretch of the imagination, but at least it was some nourishment.

He thought briefly about being back in prison. It was weird to think that he'd been there only yesterday. At least then he had been well fed and cool in the air-conditioning.

Wait a minute. Man, what am I thinking about? He chastised himself, remembering all the times he'd almost gone stir crazy with being locked up. At least out here he had the blue sky overhead and a sense of freedom. He focused his attention on the task at hand and kept moving forward, pushing on. But the going was slow, the loose sand hard to walk in.

Finally he couldn't take it any longer. He looked up ahead for a place to rest and saw a clump of bushes clinging to the side of the bank about fifty yards away. He slogged forward and in about five minutes he was there, collapsing in the shade, nearly delirious from hunger, thirst and exhaustion.

Later he figured he probably had passed out. But that was the least of his problems, because when he awoke, he heard a buzzing, rattling sound. *What the hell?* he was wondering as he rolled to his left, unfortunately surprising not only himself, but a reptile common to that part of the country – a big prairie rattler about three feet long that had sought respite from the heat in the same shade as Colby. Startled, he rolled away from the snake and, as he did so, the rattler coiled and struck him in the fleshly muscle in the back of his left arm.

He screamed and scrambled down the bank waving his arm making sure the snake was off. It was. It had slithered into the bushes for protection. Colby could hear it. The buzzing of its rattles was loud and it was freaking him out. He hated snakes almost beyond reason. That was why he grabbed his rifle, levered a shell into the chamber and fired a shot into the bushes.

It was then that the venom of the snake bite hit him and hit him hard. He collapsed on the sand, the snake still rattling away. Colby's shot had missed and it was that missed shot that the three men heard back at the other end of the gully where the dry wash started.

After Lightfoot had used the binoculars to convince himself that it was safe to proceed, they dropped down into the river bed and started following it in the direction of the rifle shot. Sugarfoot was straining on his leash in a way that was different from before. It was as if he was being driven by a sense of urgency.

After a few minutes, Benson pulled him up short. "Something's wrong," he said, looking from the bloodhound to the next bend in the riverbed and back again. "He's not normally like this." Benson paused, contemplating. "I think something's weird is going on up there," he indicated the direction they were heading.

"Weird, as in what way?" Lightfoot asked. He had learned over the years to trust his cousin's hunches.

"I'm not sure." Benson crouched down and took Sugarfoot's head gently in his hands and looked him straight in the eye. "If you could talk, fella, what would you say?"

Sugarfoot gave a muffled "woof" and in an instant

pulled away out of Benson's hands and took off at a dead run down the riverbed, trailing his leash, sand flying out behind him.

"Damn," Benson said, getting to his feet and glancing towards Lightfoot and Farley. "Let's hit it, men," he said, starting to run. "That dog is definitely on to something."

Their pace slowed to a jog and then to a fast walk by the time they made it to the first bend. Running in the sand was impossible, the footing non-existent. They did the best they could, with sweat streaming down their faces, their shirts soaking wet.

Up ahead, Sugarfoot had started to cry, a long mournful howl. He kept it up. Benson, panting, said to Lightfoot and Farley, "He only does that when he's in some sort of distress."

"Like what?" Lightfoot panted.

"The last time, he was injured. A fight with a damn coyote."

"He was okay, though, right?" Farley spoke up, just as winded as Lightfoot.

"Oh, yeah," Benson said. "But that coyote wasn't." His smile was grim. "Could be something like that."

Farley could tell Benson was worried and that worried him. He looked at Lightfoot who just motioned him onward, like, 'Just drop it.' So he did.

The howling didn't let up, but it did tell them where Sugarfoot was. They were getting closer, and Benson forged ahead. Lightfoot and Farley struggled to keep up only occasionally thinking to look out for Colby. And his rifle.

It turned out that they didn't have to worry about the fugitive. Benson rounded a curve in the river bed and was the first one to see Colby, fifty yards ahead, lying in the sand, arms outstretched, baking in the sun. Sugarfoot was by his side, like he was guarding him. "Hurry up," Benson motioned to Farley and Lightfoot. "I see him. He's not moving." Benson saw his bloodhound give Colby a lick on the face. *What the hell's going on?* he thought to himself, and ran forward as fast as he could. In less than a minute he was at the man's side.

"What's wrong with him?" Lightfoot asked as he joined his cousin.

Benson was examining the prone body. "I can't tell. Wait," he suddenly noticed something near the bushes. A dead snake. Mangled. "Geez, look at that," he pointed it out to the other two. "A rattler."

"What the hell?" Lightfoot carefully went over and examined it. "Looks like something really tore into it." Then he stopped and looked at the dog. "Would Sugarfoot do something like this?"

"Yeah, he would," Benson said, nodding and looking with affection at the panting dog. "What did you do, boy? You try and save this guy?" Sugarfoot just looked from Benson back to Colby and back to Benson, who smiled. "Yeah, maybe you did. Well let's see what we can do." Benson took off his pack. "I've got a snake bite kit here," he said to Lightfoot. "Let's get some anti-venom in him and see if we can stabilize him."

While Benson worked on Colby, Lightfoot took Farley aside. "You get to some high ground and call Hutchinson. See if we can get some assistance down here." Lightfoot placed a hand on Farley's shoulder. "Better hurry. A snake bite is a tricky thing. Some people handle it better than others." He looked at Colby. "Poor sod. Let's see if we can get him to pull through this."

Farley nodded, adrenaline starting to kick in. He hurriedly climbed out of the dry wash and was soon gone from sight, jogging as best he could towards high ground.

Benson said, "Let's see if we can get some water in him." The two men did all they could to help keep Colby alive, Sugarfoot by their side the whole time, nuzzling the unconscious fugitive, occasionally licking him. Benson cut some brush and used the branches to try and provide some shade. Lightfoot soaked a bandana and bathed Colby's face with it, trying to cool him off. Benson kept patting his dog. "Take it easy there, boy, we're doing all we can." Sugarfoot whined and kept close to the fugitive, now fighting for his life.

When Farley got back Colby was barely breathing, but he was holding on. "They're sending a helicopter," Farley panted, out of breath and sliding down the slope into the dry wash. "Can it land in here?"

"No chance," Lightfoot said. "We'll have to get him out of here." He checked his watch. "How long will it take before the chopper arrives?"

"It's coming from Medora. Shouldn't take but thirty minutes."

"Let's hurry up, then."

The helicopter was there in twenty five minutes. The men were waiting for it along the rim of the dry wash. They helped load Colby inside. Alongside the pilot was a paramedic who would administer additional first aid to Colby on the trip to the nearest hospital a hundred miles away in Dickenson. The helicopter took off leaving behind a cloud of dust that quickly disappeared in the wind. Lightfoot, Farley, Benson and Sugarfoot watched it fade in the distance, until it was just a speck. Then it was gone.

Finally, stretching and relieving some of the day's built up tension, Lightfoot said, "Well, boys, let's head on out of here."

And that's what they did, back tracking across the plains, making pretty good time since they knew exactly

60

where they were going, getting to their vehicles about an hour before sunset. As Farley told Lesley later that night after he'd showered and was on his third glass of iced tea, it had been one heck of a day.

Colby beat the odds and recovered. After a few days in the hospital he was sent back to jail in Bismarck to await trial for stealing the car.

"Benson was impressed that the guy recovered," Lightfoot told Farley when he'd heard the news. "Not everyone can survive a bite like that."

Farley nodded his head, thinking back to the chase across the plains, then asked, "How's Sugarfoot?"

"Fine, I guess. Those two are always happy when they can save someone, even if it's a career criminal like our pal Colby."

Farley laughed. "Got some problems, that one, don't you think?"

"Oh, yeah," Lightfoot said, and then changed the subject. "Let's keep working on those reports. Hutchinson's waiting for them."

And that might have been it, as far the case regarding Colby was concerned, but it wasn't.

Six months later Lightfoot and Farley were on a call that took them out to the rancher on the Little Missouri Trail who had reported the Black Honda that had turned out to be the car stolen by Colby. This time he had called in about some sort of juvenile delinquent behaviour which ended up being teenagers on his property tearing around on four-wheelers scaring his cattle.

After assuring the rancher that they'd take care of it, Lightfoot asked Farley if he wanted to drive out to where the chase had started, where Colby had gotten the stolen car stuck in the sand. Farley, said, "Sure," so Lightfoot had driven them out to where they could look over the prairie grasslands leading down to the Little Missouri River.

He parked the car and they got out. It was a bright day in December with the temperature hovering around ten degrees. Wind had scoured the land free of snow. They looked around, taking in the desolate view, squinting in the bright sun and stomping their feet to keep them warm before getting back in the car. Lightfoot started up the engine and turned the heater on. Being out where the chase had occurred got Farley wondering.

"Do you ever hear from Benson?" he asked.

"I do, occasionally. Why?"

"I was just wondering how our buddy Sugarfoot was doing."

Lightfoot smiled. "Just fine. Benson told me that they're just hunkered in for the winter. Sugarfoot spends most of the time sleeping by the fireplace. For a dog, I guess it means he's pretty happy." Lightfoot rolled up a cigarette and lit it, cracking the window to let the smoke out. "Here's a funny thing, though."

"What?"

"Benson told me that Sugarfoot has kind of taken a liking to Colby."

Farley was confused. "How did Benson know that?"

"Well, you know those two."

"Something unique between them, right?" Farley answered smiling. Benson and Sugarfoot really did seem pretty special together.

"Yeah. Well, get this. Benson has started taking Sugarfoot to Bismarck to visit Colby in prison on visiting days. They go once or twice a month. I guess Sugarfoot really likes it." Lightfoot shook his head, smiling. "That's quite the dog, I'll tell you that."

Farley nodded, thinking back to what it was like being

with Benson and Sugarfoot on that day early last summer tracking Colby across the plains. It was a day he'd never forget. They'd not only caught Colby but had saved his life. Couldn't ask for a better outcome than that.

"Well, let's get out of here," Lightfoot said, looking to the north and west, crumbling out his cigarette and tossing it out of the window into the wind. "Looks like snow is on the way."

"Sounds good," Farley said, sitting back while Lightfoot turned the car around to head back to the interstate.

"One other thing," Lightfoot said, as he started off slowly, bumping along the rough gravel road. "Benson said you were welcome to come visit them at his ranch if you wanted."

"He did? Why's that?"

"He thought you might want to see Sugarfoot."

Farley thought about it for a moment. "You know, I just might. I kind of miss him."

Lightfoot smiled. "I thought you'd say that. Benson thought you might, too."

"Next you're going to tell me Sugarfoot thought that, also," Farley said, grinning.

Lightfoot laughed. "Well, you just never know with that dog. You just really never know."

And Farley felt he knew exactly what Lightfoot was taking about.

Colby Stackhouse had been sentenced to spend the next fifteen years of his life behind bars back in Bismarck. He was kept in a prison cell in the older section of the penitentiary with three other inmates, sharing two sets of bunk beds. He wouldn't be free until he was forty seven years old. But something had happened to Colby that day when he was making his run across the grassland plains surrounding the Little Missouri River. He had almost died. That snake bite had almost done him in. If it hadn't been for those two Indians and that young highway patrolman and the dog, he'd be gone from this world. At least that's what he told anyone who'd listen to him.

"Man," he'd say, "it was like I saw my life passing before my eyes. And that life wasn't anything to be proud of."

Most everyone would roll their eyes. Even the counsellors he talked with had a tough time believing him. Colby was a lifelong criminal with a past that spoke for itself. Lying was ingrained in him. Part of his makeup.

Like one counsellor said, "You never know. He might have changed, but I doubt it. I kind of think it's in his genes. He's just a bad guy. Not the most trustworthy human being out there."

Which may have been right. Colby's story is still being written. But the funny thing is, when he gets those visits from Benson and Sugarfoot, everyone sees that there is a change happening. The dog is affectionate toward Colby and Benson talks with him like he's just a regular guy. So who knows?

From Colby's standpoint all he'll tell you is this, "You know, when I was out there in the sand, dying from that rattler's bite, that dog was right there with me. I remember coming to for just a few moments, and he licked me and kind of nuzzled my face. I know it sounds weird, but I got the feeling he didn't want me to die. Just before I passed out again, I saw him looking at me. Something about those eyes, man. They just bore into me and gave me the strength to hang in there."

When Colby talked like that most of the inmates either walked away shaking their heads or else kind of laughed, embarrassed for him. He'd been beaten up for it a few times, too. Others gave him a hard time and wrote him off as just plain nuts. But if Benson and Sugarfoot could overhear the way he talked, they'd get it. They understood that there was something special there between them and Colby. Even if they couldn't put their finger on it, it was worth pursuing. Benson and Sugarfoot would be coming to visit Colby for a long, long time. To them it seemed like the right thing to do. There was something there that needed finding out.

The grassland plains in the southwest part of North Dakota still roll off to the far distant horizon. The Little Missouri River still winds it path north to the larger Missouri. There are deeper truths out there that touch us through the spirit of the land and the voice of the wind. Benson and Sugarfoot understand that. Maybe, now, in time, Colby will too.

Sketching Snowflakes

Back then, back when he was just a gangly kid and before he became an artist, I felt I had a job to do – teach my son to be better at sports than I ever was. I'd been a second string jock during high school so on the day Joey was born I vowed to get him to learn how to play football, baseball, basketball and hockey better than I'd ever been able to. My underlying thought was that maybe one day he'd become a superior athlete, someone I could be not only proud of, but could also brag about to anyone who would listen. You can imagine my horror, (or maybe not, but let me tell you, it was real) when Joey, try as he might, proved to be even less athletically gifted than his old man.

He was nine years old the last time we went to the rink. "Dad, I know I can do better," he told me before tryouts for the hockey team that year, "watch me."

He pushed away from the boards, took two strides and promptly fell flat on his butt, sliding across the ice. He scrambled to his skates and tried to glide off but fell again, hockey stick flying through the air. He fumbled for his stick and then on his hands and knees turned to me, gritted his teeth and yelled, "Don't worry, Dad. I can do it!" He struggled to stand, but then fell again, hockey stick flying once more.

By this time the rest of the players had stopped their activities and were watching. Joey didn't seem to notice. All he wanted to do was to please me.

My heart went out to him. I stepped through the door to the rink to help, but my boots slipped out from under me and I flew up in the air, hanging suspended for what seemed like eternity before plummeting and hitting the ice hard, knocking the wind out of me. I lay flat on my back for a moment trying to catch my breath.

In the background I could hear laughter. Then I felt a hand reach out and touch my arm. "Dad? Dad are you okay?"

Joey had crawled over to check on me. "Yeah, son. I am," I said, my breath slowly returning. I looked at him. His eyes were full of concern and his forehead was furled. He cared more about me than himself. We helped each other stand up, both of us nearly falling again. "Let's go," I said.

We made our way slipping and sliding to the boards, left the ice and sat on the bench for a few minutes, each of us catching our breath and watching the rest of the skaters.

Finally Joey turned me and said, "Dad, I'm sorry, I really am. I'm trying, but those other guys are just way better than me."

One look at the fluid motions of the other kids on the rink, skating comfortably backwards better than Joey could ever skate forwards, and I had to finally admit it – my son was not, nor would ever be, a hockey player. Which was his best sport -football, baseball and basketball? Forget about it. The reality of the situation was painfully apparent. Joey would never be the star athlete I once imagined him to be.

I swallowed my disappointment and put my arm around his thin shoulders, hugging him a little. "That's okay, son. Really. Let's head home," I told him, trying to man up, along with beginning to adjust my game plan for him. Now that sports were out of the picture what could I get him interested in? Chess, maybe? Cribbage? Orienteering? I drew a blank. None of them sounded too exciting.

I went into the locker room with him while he changed out of his gear. When we sat on the bench, he unzipped his equipment bag and I saw a notebook.

I pointed. "What's that?"

"Oh, nothing," he shrugged. "It's just my sketchbook from art class."

"Art class? You're kidding." I hadn't a clue. Having trouble drawing stick figures, myself, I'd never once imagined he'd enjoy anything like painting.

He grinned. "Yeah, Dad, for my drawings. Here, let me show you." He opened it. "Lately, I've been sketching snowflakes and winter scenes. I'm thinking about maybe using them for cards for the holidays. Tell me what you think."

He lay the sketchbook on my knees and went about getting changed. I paged through his drawings, each one more impressive than the previous. He'd used what looked to be a pen and ink to create intricate snowflakes all with six pointed tips. Each one was unique and amazingly detailed. The snowflake sketches were followed by a series of charcoal drawings of winter scenes, mostly landscapes in the country, some with farmhouses, some with people, some with animals. One even had a horse drawn sleigh. He'd used coloured pencils to make the scenes come alive with subtle tones of greens and browns and reds and blues. To my way of thinking they were utterly charming and made me think of those Currier and Ives calendars.

I turned to him. "Joey, these are amazing! How long have you been drawing like this?"

He laughed. "Ever since I can remember, Dad. Since I was a little kid." Then he was quiet for a moment before adding, "Mom kind of got me started."

Oh. Gail. My wife and Joey's mother. She'd passed away four years earlier when he was only five. In many ways we were still coping.

I looked at him seriously. "These really are wonderful, son," I told him.

"Thanks, Dad," he said as we stood up to leave.

He grabbed his heavy hockey bag, hoisted it over his shoulder, tilting to the right a little under its weight, and started for the door. I held his sketchbook in my hands, aware that I was holding something special, something that really was what my son was all about, not just some sad, preconceived sports fantasy of his father's. I suddenly had an idea. "Hold on a minute." He stopped and I took the bag from him. (It really was pretty heavy.) "How about if on the way home we stop at Blick's Art Supply and check out what they've got, maybe get you some supplies. What do you think about that?"

Joey picked up his hockey stick and looked at me questioningly. He knew how much I loved sports. "You sure, Dad?"

"Yeah," I said, biting a metaphorical bullet. "Looks like we've got an artist in the family."

Joey grinned as we walked to the car. His step seemed lighter, somehow, like a weight had been lifted, and I don't just mean the equipment bag. It was good to see him so happy.

Next to the art store was a sporting goods exchange. We parked and while Joey went inside and looked around for art supplies, I went next door to see if I could sell his hockey equipment, which I did. Then I hurried next door to meet him. But before I went inside I stopped a minute, looked through the window and watched as he perused the aisles, happily caressing the paints and brushes and sketchpads and canvases. He seemed in another world, one that he felt comfortable in. Natural.

I headed for the front door. Once inside, I'd get him to show me what all the art supplies were used for. Maybe I'd buy him an easel or something to get him set up properly for his art work. He was a good kid. I guess I had a lot to learn. It was time I started paying better attention.

Blood Work

I watched the blood swirling around in the sink. *My God, there's a lot of it,* I thought to myself. *Way more than I expected.* I took hold of the bar of soap, lathered my hands and kept washing them, extra vigorously this time, trying to get more of the blood off. The bright red colour running down the drain looked like the aftermath of my ill-advised decision to let my son choose the colour of his bedroom walls many years ago. "I'd like blood red, Dad," he'd said at the time. "Like a vampire." I had agreed at the time, much to the disappointment of my wife. And anger. I never did get that roller brush clean. And, as I recall, it took three coats of Glidden's Sea Green semi-gloss to cover it all. Plus the entire next two weekends.

Anyway, the blood wasn't washing away very quickly. *Where did it all come from?* I'd read a lot of books on crime. In fact, I was sort of a student of the macabre, so I knew that the human body contained around a gallon and a half of the stuff, about the size of the bucket you might use to wash your car, and it seemed like that's the amount I was washing off my hands. *Man, I'd never expected there to be so much.*

I was in the bathroom, right off the kitchen. The sink was porcelain and the raspberry juice red of the blood contrasted with the sink's sparkling white. I wondered briefly if the blood would stain it. Shit. One more thing to worry about.

The more I washed and tried to clean my hands, the more of a mess I seemed to be making. Blood was splattering everything: up around the faucets, against the white tile backsplash and down the sides of the sink, dripping onto the pristine white tile floor. *Geez, I'd be cleaning up forever.*

I glanced in the mirror as I washed. My face looked every bit its age of seventy-one. My eyes were tired looking, bags drooping underneath. The hair on my head was thin, nearly gone, my beard was wispy and scraggly. I looked exactly like the kind of guy who would be washing blood from their hands after committing a violent crime. Not the best image to be confronted with at this stage of my life.

Suddenly, there was a pounding on the door. Bam! Bam! Bam!

"Grandpa! Grandpa! What are you doing in there?"

A grin appeared on my haggard face. "There's no one here," I said, talking to the closed door, still scrubbing furiously. "No one here but us vampires."

I heard giggles on the other side from Lari and Lori, my nine-year old twin granddaughters. It was Thursday afternoon, my day to stay with them after school until my son and his wife got home from work.

Lori called out, "Grandpa, please, please, please, what are you doing?"

"Yeah," Lari said. "Tell us, tell us, tell us."

I decided to come clean (pun intended) and tell them. "I'm washing off that blood we got at the hobby store. I'm sort of making a mess in here."

"You mean fake blood, don't you, Grandpa?" said Lori. "It was fake blood that we bought."

"Let us see. Please, let us see," Lari called out. Then, more pounding. Bam! Bam! Bam!

I could picture them jumping up and down outside the door in joyful glee. It made my heart glad. They were good kids. I cast a quick glance at myself in the mirror. At the sound of their voices, I swear my eyes became brighter and the bags under them seemed less, well, baggy. Even my beard seemed fuller. My granddaughters had that way about them, making me feel younger. Looking younger? Well, that surely was all in my imagination.

"Just a second." I grabbed some paper towels from under the sink and dried off my hands, leaving red smears and smudges all over the place. "Come on in," I opened the door.

The girls were identical red heads with long hair, green eyes, freckles, the whole bit. One thing they enjoyed doing together was playing practical jokes. Today after they'd gotten home from school we'd gone to our favourite store, Phil's Magic Emporium, and made some purchases. The plan was that we were going to surprise their parents when they got home from work today with something to do with fake blood. We'd also bought some other things.

The girls looked at the mess in the bathroom and let out a collective "Yuck!"

"I know," I said. "I think the fake blood is going to be too much of a mess to work with. What do you two think?"

While the girls pondered my question, I gave them each some paper towels, got some spray cleaner and we cleaned out the sink as well as everything else within a five foot radius. I ended up using a lot of spray bleach. A lot of paper towels, too.

When we were done, Lori said, "I think you're right, Grandpa. I don't think Mom or Dad with would like the blood. It's too messy."

"But we did get some other stuff at the store. Remember Grandpa," Lari said, starting to get excited all over again.

"Yeah, we did. They are so cool. Should I go get them Grandpa? Should I?" Lori asked.

I'd been so busy trying to clean up the fake blood I'd forgotten. I'd let each of the kids pick out something else, just in case the blood idea didn't work out, which obviously it didn't.

I played along, joking with them, "I'm getting old and forgetful. What else was it we bought again?" I scratched my chin to emphasize my forgetfulness.

The girls ran into the kitchen, giggling and pulling me along. On the counter was a shopping bag and they opened it, each taking out a treasured purchase.

"Here, Grandpa," Lori said, holding up a rubber slab of fake vomit.

"Here's mine," Lari said, taking out a clump of fake dog poop.

I laughed. They were just the kinds of things I'd have bought way back when I was their age.

I warmed up to the task at hand. "Those each will really surprise your parents," I told them, laughing.

They both grinned back at me. "Will you help us put them someplace, Grandpa?" asked Lari.

"Please, Grandpa," Lori said. "Some place special. Pretty please?"

"You bet I will," I told them. "Let's go find a couple of really good places."

"Goody, goody," they both said in unison.

Then they each took me by the hand and off we went. We took our time until we were satisfied.

Their father was home first and he was truly surprised later that evening.

"Dad," My son called from upstairs where'd he'd gone to change. "What's this in the corner of our bedroom?" The girls and I started giggling. That's where we'd put the fake dog poop. Then we heard a yell, "God-damn it, what the...?"

I guess he didn't like the fake vomit we'd lain on the quilt in the middle of the bed. The girls and I looked at each other and shrugged. Then we grinned. Oh, well, it was fun while it lasted.

In the end he didn't take it too badly. But he'd had a long day at work and wasn't in the best of moods, certainly not for fake dog-poop and vomit. All things considered we probably deserved what we got. He grounded all three of us from the Magic Emporium for the next six weeks. But what the heck, it was worth it.

The Anniversary

The bartender set a beer and a shot in front of Darren Montgomery and said, "That's it Big D. No more. I'm cutting you off after this."

Darren looked up with blurry eyes and said, "Come on Billy my boy. Can't a guy have any fun anymore?"

Except it came out as drunken gibberish, ComonBilimabycnagyhanyfumamyor?"

"I said no more drinks, Darren. You're done."

Shit. Ok. Fine, Darren wanted to say but couldn't make his mouth move to say the words. Instead, he mutely savoured the last of his whiskey and drank his beer.

He felt pretty good. Great, in fact. He'd been at the Black Crow Bar in the small town of Orchard Lake since around five that afternoon and it was now nearly eleven. He scratched his beard, happy that he'd accomplished exactly what he'd wanted to accomplish – got himself nice and wasted. To hell with his job, to hell with his wife, and to hell with his kids. He deserved a night off to forget about it all and that's exactly what he'd done. *Good for me*, he thought to himself. *Friggin' good for me.*

A short while later with the whiskey finished and beer drained he decided it was time to head home. He was making a move to stand up and go outside to where his car was parked when he leaned a little too far to the left and started to fall. From a table a few feet away a tall, thin man stood quickly and reached out a hand to steady him.

"Easy there, buddy. I've got you."

The bartender said, "You know this guy? You know Darren? I think he needs help. I was about ready to call him a cab."

The skinny guy adjusted his thick framed glasses, put his arm around Darren's shoulder and said, "Don't worry about it; he's a neighbour of mine. I've got him. I'll make sure he gets home all right." The bartender waved okay and went back to serving other patrons.

"Come on, there, partner. Let's get you out of here."

The skinny guy's name was Cody Kline. He kept his arm tight on Darren's shoulder as he manoeuvred the unsteady drunk through the bar, out the front door and into the soft warmth of an early June night. In the background frogs called from down near the lake. A moon was rising to the east and there was a sweet scent of honeysuckle in the air. Most people would have considered it a beautiful evening. Most, but not Cody Kline. He didn't notice the night at all. Instead, he propped Darren against his hip and led him across the gravel parking lot and out to the street where he'd parked his small RV.

"Let's get you inside, pal," Cody said, as he opened the door and mostly carried Darren up the two steps and into the tiny space that was the living area.

Maybe it was the change of scene that caused Darren to begin to come out of his alcoholic fog. "What? What the...?" He looked around. The space was dark, lit only by the off lighting of the street lamps. "Where am I?"

Cody set Darren on the bed, closed the curtains and turned on a tiny overhead light. "Don't worry, friend. You'll be okay. There's nothing to worry about."

Then he plunged a hypodermic needle into the man's thigh. "Hey," Darren said before his eyes glazed over and his body went numb. In a few moments he had completely passed out.

Cody gently held the back of the man's head and lay him down on the bed. Then he set about getting ready. He laid a plastic sheet on the floor, just in case there was too much blood. He went to the cabinet above his small sink, took out his tool kit and set it on the plastic sheet. He set a bright portable lamp next to the sheet and affixed a miner's light around his head. He put on his rubber gloves.

When he was satisfied all was the way he wanted it, he pulled Darren down to the sheet and arranged him on his back. He opened the man's shirt, taking a moment to notice the smooth hairless chest.

Cody smiled to himself. *Good. I won't have to shave him.*

Then he opened his tool kit and set to work. It took about half an hour. There wasn't much blood, not that he cared, but it was less to clean up. That was always a good thing.

While he moved the needle gun back and forth across the man's chest, Cody thought about his beloved son and the accident that occurred four years earlier. Ethan had been only seven years old when he'd been run over while riding his bicycle on a warm summer's evening down a quiet street near their home. He'd been killed instantly.

From that day on, the lives of Cody and his wife Samantha and four year old daughter Becky had been changed forever. He could still recall too vividly the blood smeared fragments of a twisted blue bicycle frame reflecting the flashing white lights of the ambulance at the chaotic scene. The drunk's blood alcohol content had been twice the legal limit. He was given seven years in prison. He could rot there forever as far as Cody was concerned.

God, how he'd loved Ethan. Still did. From the day he was born there'd been an instant bond between father and son starting the moment he'd held the tiny baby in his arms. While growing up, Cody had taken it upon himself to be by his boy's side as much as he could, caring for him and teaching him everything from tying his shoes and learning to read, to creating Lego models and how to ice skate. Ethan had been the light of his life, his reason for living. With his death, though, Cody had been damaged deep inside on every level, finding it impossible to fill the void left by the loss of his son. For weeks afterwards, he lived in a fog, emotionally crippled.

He almost lost his job. Cody was a high school art teacher, and as much as he loved teaching, he'd lost the will to get himself to school and stand in front of a class. He was granted a leave of absence and was given three months off. It didn't help. His relentless grief continued to hang over him like a shroud. When the time came to return to his classes he forced himself to go, taking up where he'd left off, teaching introductory drawing to ten graders, determined to do his best. In some small way he felt that it's what Ethan would have wanted.

Who knows how long things would have stayed that way if not for a student in Cody's drawing class who, soon after his return, brought in a poster from the novel, *The Girl with the Dragon Tattoo*. Cody was immediately enthralled with the detail of the design, the subtle colours and flow of the lines. From that moment on his life started to turn around. He loved the artwork of the tattoo on the poster so much so that he not only started making his own drawings, he signed up for a class and learned the art of tattooing.

Cody's wife Samantha was ecstatic to see her husband become more whole again, or, as she put it, "Back to his old self." She was a registered nurse and worked at a hospital the next town over. She was a strong, self-reliant person and over the months had learned to accept the loss of their son. She'd moved on and was glad to see Cody was on the way to healing as well.

As the anniversary of the first year of Ethan's death approached, Cody came up with an idea and discussed with it Samantha. She listened intently. When he was finished he said, "I need to do this, honey. I think Ethan would appreciate it."

Samantha wasn't sure about Ethan, but she had a feeling

her husband needed to do what he was proposing. "Well, I think it's an insane idea, but I also think I understand why you need to do it." She took him by the shoulders and looked him in the eyes and told him, "Go ahead." Then she hugged him and added, "Just be careful and make sure you come home safely to us."

"I will," he sighed with relief, happy she understood, and held her tight. "I will."

Cody's idea was to use his skill as a tattoo artist to make a statement. He bought an old RV and fixed it up in preparation for what was to become a yearly ritual.

That was three years ago.

When he had finished working on Darren, Cody directed the light and peered closely. He dabbed some blood away with an antiseptic cloth and took a moment to admire his work. He'd used his tattoo needle to print, `I will never ever drive drunk again`. It took up a large portion of the man's chest.

"This looks good," he said out loud, studying the fresh tattoo. "You should be proud, jerk. It's the best work I've ever done." The comatose man didn't bat an eye.

Cody put his tools away, cleaned up and tossed his blood stained gloves in the trash. He waited until the streets were empty before dragging the unconscious man outside and hid him in the bushes by the side of the bar, figuring that the guy would come around by sunrise. Then he got in the RV and left town, already feeling the energized rush he always received when a tattooing was completed. It was a feeling he could get used to.

He pointed his RV down the single lane highway and drove east, bright headlights cutting through the summer night, heading home to Samantha and Becky. The clock on the dash read four in the morning. He'd be with them in less than twelve hours. He couldn't wait.

An hour from home he pulled into a wayside park and turned off the RV. He climbed into the back and took out his needle gun. He pulled up his shirtsleeve and exposed a tattoo on his left forearm; a tattoo he'd inked when he was first learning. It read *Ethan Lives* in black letters that were enclosed in a bright pink heart. Underneath were three smaller hearts, one for each year since his son's death, one for each tattoo he'd etched onto the chest of an unsuspecting drunk. When his gun was ready, he made a fourth one.

Then he put his equipment away and started up the RV and headed for home. As he drove he dabbed away some blood from his newly tattooed heart. The pain didn't bother him; it made him feel more alive. He was already looking forward to one year from now, another anniversary, another tattooed drunk and another chance to show his son that he'd never forget him. It was the least he could do.

Don't Slip and Fall

It was mid-January and sunny, with a temperature about fifteen degrees, as good a day as you could ask for to be outside. "I'm going for my walk," I told Eve. "I'll be back in half an hour."

"Don't slip and fall," my wife called back.

She was in the kitchen stirring a pot of homemade chicken noodle soup. It smelled good enough to keep me inside. Almost. I'm a little compulsive on some things and my late morning walk in the winter is one of them. "I'll be careful."

"It just snowed you know, Rick. You usually fall at least two or three times a year and haven't yet, so you're due. Watch yourself."

Snowfall had been intermittent this winter so walking had been fairly easy. I opened the door to a blast of cold air. "I will," I said, stepping outside. "Besides, it's only a dusting," I added, shutting the door quickly before she could caution me again. Hell, I was sixty-five and certainly old enough to know what I was doing.

Well, sort of. First off, it was more than a dusting, closer to an inch, so I made myself walk cautiously as I started out. Even so, I'd slipped once or twice by the time I had reached the end of the driveway. At least I hadn't fallen. Man, I really did need to be careful.

I turned right and made my way down our quiet street, snow crunching underfoot, glad for my warm jacket, insulated boots, heavy mittens and wool cap. My wife's words echoed like a bad mantra in my head, *Don't slip and fall. Don't slip and fall.* It was hugely irritating, made even more so by the fact that she was right; I usually did slip and fall two or three times a year. So I took it as a challenge. No slipping and falling. Not today.

Except I did.

I was rounding the corner at the end of the block thinking about not slipping when I stepped on clean patch of snow. Underneath there must have been a smooth sheet of ice because all of a sudden my feet shot out from under me and I fell backwards, completely air born. For a moment I hung suspended in space, my eyes for some reason locked onto a jet contrail cutting across the blue sky above. I should have used that time to prepare myself to cushion my backside when I hit the ground, but didn't. What I thought, as I reached the top of the arc and began plummeting towards earth, was: *Damn it. She was right again.*

I smacked my head hard on the pavement. Fortunately, I wasn't knocked out but, instead, ended up lying slightly stunned on the snowy street. A neighbour saw the whole thing and called Eve who drove over to get me. Then she hurried me to the clinic to get me checked out before taking me home.

She got me situated on the couch with a steaming bowl of her chicken noodle soup on a tray on my lap before sitting next to me. "I'm glad the doctor told us you're going to be all right," she said, gently caressing my head. "But, I worry about you so much, Rick. I understand that you like your winter walks, I just don't want you to hurt yourself." She paused, then added, "I just wish you'd be more careful and maybe stay inside when the weather's bad." She gave me a quick, wifely kiss on the forehead. It felt wonderful.

I savoured the soup thinking that of course her words made sense. We'd been married for forty-two years and one thing I knew for a certainty was that everything my wife did or said made sense. I should have known that fact by now but apparently was too mule-headed to accept it.

I'm sure there was resignation all over my voice when I said, "Yeah, I know what you're saying, Eve. I'll think about it." I finished my soup then closed my eyes, suddenly very tired. I knew what she was saying, but still it didn't change the fact that some habits were hard to change. My winter walk, apparently, was one of them.

Eve set the tray and my empty bowl aside and helped my lie down. Then she stood up and patted my arm affectionately. "You do that. In the meantime, I'll go wash this out. You rest. We'll have some more later for dinner. Okay?" She went into the kitchen after tucking a thick quilt around my legs to keep me warm.

I awoke an hour later and looked out of the window. Snow was falling steadily and the afternoon light was fading from the sky. I watched the flurries swirl as the wind picked up. My guess was that the temperature was getting colder and I wondered if maybe I should skip my walk tomorrow. Like Eve had said, I usually fell two or three times a year. Today's fall was my first and simple math told me that I was due for one or two more. Next time I could get seriously injured. Tomorrow I should stay inside, take it easy and baby that bump on my head. A wise man would do that, right? Well, no one ever accused me of being wise. Just ask Eve.

I could hear her puttering in the kitchen, rattling some pots and pans. The aroma of chocolate chip cookies baking drifted out to where I was lying. I could just make out the melody of a song she was humming, *Greensleeves*. A new year had begun but Eve was still imbued with the Christmas Spirit. I was a lucky man. She was a good person and a wonderful wife. It didn't take a genius to realize that I had been right about one thing all those years ago. I'd been right to propose to her. It was the smartest thing I ever did.

Maybe tomorrow I should stay in and take it easy like she suggested. Watch the snow and have some more of that tasty soup. And a cookie. Yeah, that sounded like a good idea. There was a very good possibility I might slip and fall. Better to be safe than sorry.

Hey, look at me after all these years doing what Eve suggested! I know exactly how she'd react. She'd give me a knowing smile and say, "It's about time."

You know what? She'd be right.

The Last Time I Ran Away

I ran away from home twice.

The first time I was five years old. It was right after my sister was born and I guess I was feeling sorry for myself, what with the attention my parents were paying to her and all. I remember I put some plastic dinosaurs in my pocket, tied a cape around my neck like Superman my favourite superhero (a raggedy old towel, actually), put on my Minnesota Twins baseball hat and left home. My jerk older brother Sean just laughed at me. I got two blocks away before Mrs. Nelson, a kindly kindergarten teacher out working in her garden saw me, figured something wasn't quite right and brought me home. I don't believe I could sit down comfortably for a week after the spanking my father gave me.

The second time, seven years later, I should have known better.

"God damn it, you big bully!" I yelled at Sean.

He laughed and grabbed me in another head-lock and ground his knuckles over my skull, giving me a rub, just one more torture in his bag of tortures he was forever dishing out to me, his unfortunate little brother. Older by three years, Sean outweighed me by fifty pounds, was almost a foot taller and was becoming the horror, the absolute terror of my existence, something I certainly didn't need.

Finished with the knuckle rub he threw me to the ground, punched me in the back, rubbed my face in the dirt and walked away, whistling happily. It was just another normal day.

Mom had left home with her boyfriend the year before, never to be heard of again, leaving me and Sean and my younger sister, Lea, under the care of my poor excuse of a father and his girlfriend Sally who my dad, I kid you not, always called Sexy Sal. Geez.

Now, when I say that the two adults responsible for taking care of Sean, Lea and me left something to be desired in the parenting department, that would be putting it mildly. Dad worked for some kind of auto parts store and drove a delivery truck between our home in the little town of Orchard Lake, located twenty miles west of Minneapolis, and St. Cloud, seventy miles to the north. Sexy Sal worked at a cut rate (no pun intended) hair salon in Brooklyn Center, about thirty miles away. I think it was called the 'Cut n' Go' so you can probably imagine what it was like.

Sexy Sal wore her bleach blond hair in a bee-hive style like it was the year 1965, smoked Kool cigarettes and liked to drink any kind of beer that was available. Dad wasn't much better, but without the hair. He was a large man, a Camel straight smoker with a big beer belly who shaved his head when he started going bald ten years earlier and had grown his beard out so he looked like an outlaw biker. Maybe that was his fantasy, but who knew? All I can tell you is that he didn't own a motorcycle. That was a fact. Being an outlaw? Well, not that I knew of, but you'd have to ask him if you really wanted to know.

I'm telling you all of this to let you know they were gone from home a lot, leaving us to supervise ourselves and let me tell you, the end result wasn't pretty. Especially that summer. I guess Sean at fifteen was supposed to be in charge, but he was a mean little kid when he was young and the older he got, the meaner he became. My belief from the time I could think at all was that he was born a jerk and nothing in my life up to this point contradicted that idea.

I suppose in the long run I should have considered myself lucky to be just getting knuckle rubs from him. After all, in the beginning of the summer he had started carrying a Buck 110 folding knife with a four and a half inch blade that locked in place and the things he used to do to frogs and toads and the occasional baby bird...Man, it still makes me sick just thinking about it. It was my ever growing fear that he could easily start doing the same to me. Or worse.

Fortunately he didn't bother with my little sister Lea. I guess he thought that being a girl she wasn't much worth the time. She mostly stayed in her room and played with her dolls, smart enough to stay out of the way of her two older brothers who fought all the time and, in general, made life around the house pure hell.

Add to that the fact Dad and Sal liked to party a lot when they were home with the beer and weed...well, like I said, they weren't going to win any prizes when it came to parenting, that was for sure.

My teacher last year in sixth grade used to read to us from a book the final half hour of the day on Fridays. We ended the year with *Tom Sawyer* and I have to tell you that I liked the main character a lot. The two things I got from the book were that: one, even though Tom was a hellion (big word, huh? I might have gotten it from the book), he at least had his aunt who loved him, and two, sometimes running away was a good idea.

So that's what I did.

School had ended in early June and by the middle of July I'd had it with Sean. He was supposed to be working that summer at Jorgenson's hardware store, a place near enough to us so he could walk or ride his bike, but he kept getting to work later and later until finally Mr. Jorgenson the owner just up and fired him. I heard that his final words to Sean were, "Send Quinn back here when you get home. He's ten times the worker you are."

Now, how he knew that I had no idea, but it pissed off Sean no end and when he got back to our house he beat me up, apparently just on general principles. He must have enjoyed it too, deriving some perverse, sick pleasure in pounding me because it started him on his campaign of terror, tormenting me every day, beating me up whenever he had the chance and making my life miserable. And for no good reason, I might add, other than I was small for my age and couldn't fight back. He was just as mean to me as he always had been and getting meaner with each passing day.

I remember the last time he did it very clearly. It was a Tuesday morning and he'd caught me in the back by the garage cleaning the spokes of my bike, not paying attention or being on the lookout for him like I normally was. He jumped me from behind and pounded the crap out of me, twisting my arm up behind my back just for good measure while I begged him to stop. When he was finally done with me he threw me to the ground, stomped on my back and left me lying sprawled out in the dirt.

Then he sneered at me and said, "I'll see you later," which of course meant he'd beat me up again. Then he sauntered inside to play Final Fantasy VII on the PlayStation set up in the living room.

I sat up and wiped the blood from my nose and wondered how I was going to ever survive until school started because now with him not at work, Sean seemed to take it as his new job to torment me at will. Full time. Not a pleasant future for me at all. Fall looked to be a long time away.

You might wonder, 'Why doesn't this kid just tell his dad?' That's a very good question. I momentarily thought about it that day but had a feeling it would be as fruitless as the approximately five hundred other times I'd told him over the years – about Sean and how he made my life a living hell on a daily basis. But there never was a lot a lot of sympathy for my plight from dear old Dad on that front. "Just suck it up and deal with it, Quinn," was his basic answer, often followed up with, "Be a man, for Christssake," tacked on at the end for good measure. Thanks a lot, Dad. So no, I didn't spend a lot of time that day thinking about telling my dad anything about Sean and what he was doing to me. I figured I'd just have to find a way to learn to live with it.

I was just rousting myself to get to my feet, clamber on to my bike and go for ride to get away from that big idiot of a brother for a while, when something happened that I'll never forget. Lea quietly opened the back screen door, walked across the thread bare patch of grass we called a backyard and sat down in the dirt next to me. She was seven years old and a skinny little snip of a thing. She had long, stringy blond hair and liked to wear soft cotton dresses that probably were colourful once but were now faded away to grey after so many washings. And, like I mentioned before, she liked to stay in her room and play with her dolls. Barbie's. I think she had three of them. She and I were pretty close, maybe because of Sean. I liked her and she liked me and I even gave her rides on my bike every now and then, you know, just goofing around.

Anyway, she never talked much and she didn't this time either, but she did something then that I later thanked her for over and over and over again in the years to come. She reached her hand into the pocket of her dress, pulled out Sean's knife and handed it to me only saying, "He left it on the kitchen table. I don't think he's missed it yet." Then she got up, brushed the dirt off her dress, skipped back to the house and went inside. It was the most she'd spoken to me in I don't know how long.

Stunned, I held the knife in my hand. It had a golden brown handle and when I snapped it open its shining, razor sharp blade gleamed in the sun. Sean had brought it earlier that summer at the hardware store with his first paycheck and was as proud of it as anything else in his life, even more than the PlayStation. I knew it was only a matter of time before he noticed the knife was missing and why Lea gave it to me I could only guess. Maybe for my own protection. But if I kept it and he found out...Man, I pictured him beating me up in a way so bad that I quickly had to erase the image from my mind because it was too disturbing. Then I imagined him coming at me with his knife, using the blade on me like I'd seen him use it on those poor defenceless creatures and I shuddered at the thought.

God, why was I thinking about those kind of things right now? *Stop it!* I told myself. So I did.

But what I did think about right then and there was that now was the time to go. Now was the time to get away from this hell-hole of a life and move on to 'Greener pastures', a phrase I'd heard once in school, maybe in Tom Sawyer.

And that's exactly what I did.

I stood up, put the knife in my front pocket, crept to the back door and listened through the screen. I could hear Sean playing Final Fantasy VII so I knew what little mind he had was now completely occupied by his make believe world on the PlayStation. Good.

I quietly opened the door, holding my breath when it screeched a little, and tip-toed across the kitchen floor, glad I was wearing my converse sneakers. I crept to Lea's room and went inside, closing the door quietly behind me. She was sitting on the floor with her dolls arranged in front of her in a half circle. She looked up at me with her big eyes and greeted me with a little smile. I went to her, knelt down and gave her a hug.

"I just wanted to tell you good bye," I said, holding her tight. "I'm leaving and I'm taking the knife with me."

I couldn't think of what else to say so I sat back, looked

90

at her once and then hugged her again. She held me close and right then I almost didn't go, not wanting to leave her all by herself. But I forced myself to pull away and stand up. I quickly stepped back before I could think too much about what I was intending to do and maybe talk myself out of it. I went to her door and opened it, looking back once when I heard her say, "Be careful."

I waved to her and whispered, "I will," as I stepped out of her room, watching as she waved to me while I closed the door. With the sound of it latching in place I felt like I was not only saying goodbye to my sister, but saying goodbye to part of myself, too. I have to admit, it was pretty emotional. But since I now had the knife I had a strong reason to go or else face Sean's wrath – my desire to runaway stronger than doing the smart thing which would have been to put the knife back on the kitchen table and forget the whole thing.

Lea's image would come back to me again and again over the course of that day. Dad and Sexy Sal? I never thought of them once.

I snuck across the hall to the room I shared with Sean and reached under my mattress where I kept my wallet hidden. It had seven dollars and thirty seven cents collected from the odd jobs I did for my next door neighbour and I figured I could use the money on the road. I put it in my back pocket and then glanced in the mirror, choosing not to dwell on my small size and skinny build, concentrating instead on what I was wearing. I had on a tee-shirt that once was white but now was kind of grey, like my sister's dress, and cut off blue jeans. I wondered if I should maybe bring a jacket. *Naw*, I thought to myself, *it's too hot out. I'll get a job somewhere if I need more clothes.* The idea of traveling light appealed to me. Just like a hobo or something. I was both excited and nervous, but not that nervous. I took one last look and whispered, "Good bye forever." Then I was gone.

I snuck out of my room, down the hall, through the kitchen and out of the house. I ran to the garage, jumped on my bike and rode it through our little town out to the highway where I stopped, looking back and forth in both directions. Right would take me past the lake our town was named after and eventually all the way to the big city of Minneapolis. I really didn't want to go there, so I started riding my bike west, in the opposite direction, out towards the country. Besides, there were a lot of cars on the road going that way and I figured I had a better chance of catching a ride.

A mile of riding brought me to the outskirts of town. I hid my bike in a weed filled ditch and climbed back onto the highway. It wasn't even noon yet, but the sun was burning hot and I was already sweating. I stood on the side of the road and put my thumb out, just like I'd seen them do on the television. I had no idea where I was going or what I was going to do when I got there. All I knew was that I was running away for real this time. I felt in my front pocket. The first time I ran away I brought toy dinosaurs. This time I had Sean's knife. It gave me a sense of security and I liked that feeling. It was a feeling I wasn't used to and it felt good.

Highway 12 is a two lane road that leads west to the Minnesota boarder with South Dakota and beyond that all the way to Montana and I think eventually to the Pacific Ocean. I'd been standing there for maybe fifteen minutes when he pulled over. I'd been there long enough to get hot and sweaty and beginning to start looking longingly at the Texaco station about a quarter mile down the road, thinking maybe I could find a hose or something and get a free drink of ice cold water.

He was driving an old, faded red and slightly rusted pickup truck with a big dog kennel in the back, but no dog. There was also a roll of dark green canvas tied up with rope. I bent down and peered in the side window as the truck rolled to a stop.

He leaned across the seat toward me. "Hi there, young man. Need a lift?"

He seemed nice and polite. He was maybe thirty years old, clean shaven with light brown hair that fell across his forehead. He was wearing tan coloured slacks with a sharp crease in each leg and a clean white, short sleeved dress shirt, open at the collar. For some reason I remembered his shoes as being fancy. They had tie laces and were shiny and black. To me, coming from with a dad who was big, bearded, and scary looking, this guy looked like a choirboy. You know, someone safe.

In addition to being so hot, I had frankly started to get bored. "Sure," I said, happy to get out of the sun and trusting he was as innocent as he seemed. I opened the door. "Where're you going?" I thought to ask, not that I cared. Anywhere away from my home and Sean was good enough for me. I climbed in and settled onto the front seat.

"Anywhere you want," he joked, laughing, showing me a row of small front teeth stained brown. He put the truck in gear and carefully accelerated back onto the highway.

His response to my question seemed odd and right then and there my rather cavalier attitude about hitting the road and living on my own began to diminish. I started to get just the tiniest bit nervous. In rethinking my actions that day, I should have jumped out while I had the chance, but I was just a kid who didn't know any better.

Well, what the heck? I thought to myself. *What have I got to lose? He seems nice enough. Everything should be Ok.*

Besides, I'd made my decision to run away and that's what I was going to do. I set my suspicions aside and settled in on the bench seat of the truck thinking that I might as well enjoy my ride and whatever lay ahead, just like a real adventure.

"What's your name, young man?" he asked as he brought the truck up to speed. The wind blowing through the cab was hot, but it felt lots better than standing on the side of the highway baking to death. He had a soft voice with a kind of southern accent and seemed very well mannered.

"Quinn," I told him, wondering if I should tell him my last name was Charles. Naw, I decided not to. I'd taken enough ribbing in my life for having a first name as my last name. "What's yours?" I asked instead.

He told me his name was Ronny. "Like Ronny Milsap," he said laughing. "You know, the blind country singer?"

I had no idea what he was talking about. Dad was a big Lynard Skynard fan. Ronny Milsap? Never heard of the guy.

"Don't know him," I said.

Ronny just shrugged and grinned with those brown teeth which for some reason were starting to irritate me. How hard was it to take a minute and brush your teeth every day, anyway? Even Sean did that and he hardly had the gumption to get dressed in the morning. Plus, now that I was in the truck and even though the windows were down, there was a stink inside that was starting to make me a little sick to my stomach. Maybe it had something to do with the dog that kennel was for. But there was no dog around. To take my mind off the stink and my nausea I asked him where he was going.

"Out west, Quinn. Got a job lined up."

That sounded great. I'd never been further away from

94

home than Minneapolis, and once up north to Duluth. Out west? Never.

"What kind of job?" I asked, just to be polite.

"Anything they want me to do, young fella. I'm a self-made man. I do a little bit of this, and a little bit of that."

Well, that sounded good to me and I turned completely toward him, interested. Dad was always complaining about his job and the delivery truck he had to drive. At my young age 'Doing a little bit of this and a little bit of that' sounded like a pretty good deal.

"Does it pay good?"

He laughed long and hard at that one. "You bet it does, my boy. You bet it does."

My boy? I shifted a little in my seat. The stink was starting to go away, or maybe I was getting used to it. I looked at Ronny thinking that even though the guy seemed a little strange, all in all he seemed pretty harmless. At least he wasn't mean like Sean, or ignoring me like my dad always did. That counted for something. I felt myself relaxing a little bit more. My stomach was a little better, too. *This ride might not turn out to be so bad after all,* I thought. *In fact, it might turn out to be pretty good.*

Ronny liked to talk. "Yeah, I grew up in Oklahoma on a ranch," he said, talking loud to be heard above the wind blowing through the cab. "But I wanted to hit the road and see the world. I've worked as a cowboy on a ranch in Montana and did maintenance on an oil rig in the Gulf of Mexico. I was a forest ranger in Idaho, gold miner in Colorado and a riverboat captain on the Mississippi River."

I was impressed and enjoyed listening to him. I think he'd also been a bush pilot in Alaska and worked on a lobster boat up there, too.

So he'd done a lot and my imagination kept running away with me, picturing myself in each of those settings.

95

Despite my initial misgivings I was beginning to warm to the guy. Not once did I think for a moment that he might be making all those jobs up to impress me, relax me and get on my good side.

Around mid-afternoon we stopped at a service station in western Minnesota near the town of Benson. I got out and stretched my legs while Ronny pumped gas. The temperature had to have been around ninety. The heat reflecting off the payment was rising in rippling waves and even the tar in the parking lot felt soft under my tennis shoes. I looked west out across a big cornfield towards the horizon. There was nothing out there but more and more corn. The stalks looked shrivelled, the leaves faded. The wind blew hot from the south. The only things alive were some crows across the highway, feeding on something on the ground.

I was picturing myself swimming in a nice, cool lake somewhere, floating on an inner tube, when Ronny asked, "Quinn, are you hungry?"

His voice startled me. He'd finished with the gas and had come up beside me. He put his hand on my shoulder. I was surprised to see him not sweating at all because I really was. It was running down my back and I could feel it beading up on my forehead. I looked towards the service station still conscious of his hand on me. It felt a little strange because my dad never did stuff like that, but to be honest, it didn't feel too bad either. Next to the station was a little cafe with a red checker awning and a sign that read, *Ma's Place*. It looked inviting to me.

"Sure," I said. Visions of pancakes with butter and syrup dripping off the sides and an order of sausages filled my mind. All I'd had to eat that day was my usual breakfast of a bowl of Cheerios which I'd had to eat dry since Sean had taken the last of the milk. I suddenly realized that I was beyond hungry, I was starving. "That'd be great," I turned and smiled at him.

Ronny smiled in return and said, "Be right back." I watched as he went to the truck. I had a sudden clutching feeling that he'd take off and leave me stranded all by myself in this little town out in the middle of nowhere. But to my relief he didn't. He simply started the engine, pulled away from the pumps and parked by the cafe. Then he got out, came over to where I was standing, put his arm around my shoulder and led me inside. I had to admit, I was relieved he had stayed with me.

The cafe was air-conditioned and the cold air hit me so hard it took my breath away. We sat in a booth with red vinyl seats that were slippery but comfortable. I quickly cooled off and entertained myself watching the sweat dry on my arms. The waitress was young and, to my inexperienced eyes, really good looking. She had dark, wavy brown hair that fell past her shoulders, just like my mom used to have. She brought us an icy pitcher of water and I drank down a glass in about ten seconds, the water so cold it made the sides of my head hurt.

We sat across from each other and Ronny made small talk with the waitress whose name tag read 'Annie'. He even turned around and chatted with the people seated behind him, an elderly couple who looked to me like they had just stepped in from the farm. I tried not to stare at the ring of white around the farmer's hairline and forehead that was probably from the hat he wore when he was working outside, driving his tractor or something. The lower half of his face was deeply tanned and he wore a plaid, short sleeved shirt and a clean pair of bib blue jeans. His wife wore a pretty floral dress and a bonnet. I got the feeling this was a special outing for them. I caught a faint aroma of manure, maybe from the guy's boots, that I have to say

97

wasn't all that unpleasant. For some reason, I liked seeing them in the cafe with us.

I ordered three pancakes the size of which blew me away when Annie set them down in front of me. I think she might even have winked at me. They took up the whole plate. I drowned them in maple syrup and slabs of butter and wolfed them down along with my side order of sausages (just liked I'd imagined.) Man, they tasted fantastic. Ronny didn't order anything. He just sat and smiled at me while I ate. I was so hungry it never even occurred to me how strange it was that he didn't order or eat anything. He barely drank any water.

After I finished I excused myself to use the bathroom. When I was done, I washed my hands and splashed cold water on my face. As I was drying off I looked at my reflection in the mirror. I couldn't believe how red my face was and my freckles stood out like crazy. I was a little sheepish about my looks. Most of the boys I knew and went to school with had nice, shiny, longish hair – long enough to blow a little in the wind. Dad had something against that kind of hair, probably because he'd lost most of his, so whenever he used his electric razor to shave his head he also did me and Sean. Buzzed us right down to the scalp. So, along with being outcasts in town because of our family situation, we were also outcasts on account of how different we looked because of our hair, or lack of it so to speak. Now that I was on the road I got the idea that I'd let my hair grow out. I didn't have to think long. *Yeah, let's do that*, I thought to myself and smiled into the reflection in the mirror at my great idea. *Starting now.* Then I finished drying my hands and joined Ronny back at the table.

He greeted me with, "All set, there, Quinn?" He had been using my first name ever since I'd introduced myself when he'd first picked me up. I liked that he wasn't like my dad, who just ordered me around, getting him beers and stuff, or Sean, who didn't talk to me all, preferring instead to push me around and, of course, beat me up. Ronny talking to me was different but in a good way, like I was a real person. It was kind of nice.

"Yeah, I'm good."

He pointed to my water glass. "Drink up, my boy. We might not be stopping again for a while."

"Ok."

I dutifully finished off my water and stood up. I noticed Ronny hadn't left a tip for my pancakes and sausage. I thought about using some of my own money from my wallet, but Ronny seemed in a hurry so I didn't. He hurried me out of the cafe and hustled me to the truck. I felt bad I didn't leave the nice waitress at least a quarter.

We got in the truck and I got settled. Ronny started the engine and drove out of the parking lot onto the highway. I was pleasantly full and feeling good, thinking that running away was the smartest thing I'd ever done and that life on the road was the perfect solution to all my problems at home. But after a few minutes staring at cornfields, cows and the occasional farm house and barn, the heat must have started to get to me, because I began to feel kind of groggy. I put my hand on my forehead and was surprised that it felt cold and clammy instead of hot which was weird because I was sweating heavily under my tee-shirt.

"Quinn, are you feeling Ok?" Ronny asked, looking at me with a strange expression. One I can only describe as both concerned and excited.

"Not really," I said, feeling my words slur.

He patted the seat. "Just lay your head down here, my boy. Rest. I'm sure you'll feel better soon."

He sounded like he cared about how I was feeling so I

trusted him and did just as he suggested.

"Ok," I said. And I lay my head down.

The next thing I knew I was waking up. Well, coming to was more like it. I was lying completely stretched out across the front seat of some sort of vehicle with my head jammed under the steering wheel. I was looking at the foot well and saw a brake pedal and an accelerator pedal and a steering column and a bunch of wires. It took a minute for me to work it out, but when I did I remembered I was in Ronny's truck. Then it all started coming back to me, the hitch-hiking, the truck, Ronny, the cafe. But why was I here by myself? Where was Ronny?

I sat up and rubbed my eyes, feeling dizzy and disoriented. I looked out of the driver's side window and saw cleared spaces on the ground, grass, a few trees and some picnic tables. I looked out of the front window and saw I was about fifty feet from a big, muddy river rimmed with brush, bushes and some tall trees and it dawned on me that I had to be at a camp ground somewhere. The river looked to be about a hundred feet across and, if I had to guess, I thought it might be the Minnesota River since we'd been heading in that direction the last I knew. I looked to my right and there was Ronny standing on the bank looking out over the river.

I watched him as I took a few moments getting my bearings. I was really kind of out of it. My head felt fuzzy and it was hard to think. My mouth was dry and felt full of cotton. My eyes were caked with sleep and crap and I rubbed them as clean as I could. My stomach ached too, pretty awful, like the flu. I'd been sick bad in my life before but not much worse than this. Then my stomach heaved once and I fought back an urge to throw up. Thankfully both windows were down, not only because of potential vomiting, but also because it was still hot out and it helped to have a little air movement in the truck. I could see out the front that we were pointing west. The sun was above the trees on the other side of the river but starting to go down, its rays shining into the cab, adding to the heat. I was woozy but sitting up seemed to be helping. I was slowly starting to feel better.

For some reason I had the feeling I should be as quiet as I could be, so instead of yelling out and greeting Ronny with, "Hi there. I'm awake," I scrunched down and peered over the edge of the window, spying on him and getting a feel for my surroundings. He had set up a tent near to a picnic table. It was of those old fashioned dark green, canvas ones with no windows that looked just plain hot and it occurred to me that it must have been what I'd seen in the back of the truck when he'd first stopped for me. From my seat in the cab, which now with the sun shining in, was starting to burn a little, I carefully looked all around outside, expecting to see other campers. But the eerie thing was that I didn't see anyone else. Not a soul. Which was surprising considering it was the middle of summer and everyone in Minnesota knew this was the height of the camping season. Even me, and I'd never been camping before in my life.

Maybe that's what we were going to do, I thought. *Ronny and me were going to go camping together and that would be fun.* But it was strange that Ronny really didn't appear to be camping. He didn't have a fire going, or any firewood, or fishing poles, or a cooler or anything. All he was doing was standing and looking out at the river. What was that all about? I thought most people went fishing or something when they went camping. And the way he was acting seemed doubly odd to me, now that I thought about it, because I hadn't seen any luggage or camping gear or anything like that when he'd picked me up, other than that old roll of canvas which turned out to be the tent. Then I saw he'd put the big dog kennel next to the tent. He must have moved it there from the back of the truck. Maybe he had camping stuff in the tent, but if he did, where had it come from? I was confused and beginning to get both nervous and suspicious. What was he up to?

Just to be sure, I cautiously turned around and looked out of the driver's window and then out the back, and then it dawned on me, not only were we all alone, but I was here with this guy who all of a sudden was starting to seem kind of creepy, just like when he'd first picked me up and I'd gotten into his truck. That feeling I had back then was coming back to me all over again. My heart thumped a little in my chest. Something wasn't right.

As I scrunched down and went back to watching him over the edge of the window, he reached down, ran his right hand along his right thigh and began moving it back and forth, back and forth, back and forth. Then he casually moved it into his crotch, massaging and rubbing it, keeping his hand there for a long time, like he was playing with himself or something.

Then it hit me and a feeling of dread washed over me that made my entire body go weak. My friends at school sometimes talked about weirdos who played with themselves and other stuff. I wasn't sure if that's what he was doing right now but whatever it was it didn't seem right, and I'll tell you what, it scared the hell out of me. My heart jumped and started racing. Call it a gut feeling or a premonition or what have you, but it was same feeling I'd get when Sean looked at me a certain way, just before he started to chase me, hoping to catch me and beat me up. But this feeling I had now towards Ronny was a thousand times worse. It was a feeling of stone cold fear.

I quickly ducked down. My heart started pounding

away and a wave of terror washed over me. I had to fight back an urge to scream. Then it occurred to me that if I screamed no one would have heard me anyway and knowing I was so alone just made it worse. I was so scared, so terribly frightened. I didn't want anything bad to happen to me and I made myself hold back my fear and tried to think. I had to do something, but what? My whole body started shaking. I kept my head lowered below the window and searched in my mind for what I should do next. I came up with nothing. Absolutely nothing. I realized I was trapped. The shaking got way worse after that.

And who knows...I might have lost it right then and there and surrendered to my fate with Ronny except for one thing. My mind went to the safest place I knew, my home. I saw Dad and Sexy Sal and Sean and Lea. I focused on Lea, my sweet little sister who I cared for more than anyone else in the whole wide world. Then I remembered that Lea had given me Sean's knife. I had it in my pocket. And it wasn't so much the knife, although that was certainly comforting in a totally bizarre kind of way, but it was the thought of Lea giving it to me that helped calm me down. I centred my mind on my last vision of her, my little sister playing with her dolls, nice and safe in her bedroom, and I made myself keep that vision in my mind as I tried to reason out what I should do. There was one thing for sure. Ronny was some kind of weirdo, there was no doubt about that, just like my friends at school used to talk about. I wasn't safe and it was only a matter of time before he came for me. I had to figure out how I could get away.

My first idea was that maybe I could climb out the opposite window on the driver's side, slide to the ground and make a break for it. But then where would I go? And what if he saw me? What if I couldn't outrun him and he caught me? Then what? Oh, man, *think Quinn*, I told myself. *Think.* But I was so scared my mind was starting to go blank.

I took a chance and snuck a peek over the edge of the window frame to check on him and that was my undoing. Ronny suddenly turned away from the river and his eyes settled on me and he saw me staring at him. *God, no.* He grinned.

I froze.

"Well, well, well. Look who's awake," he said, his face breaking into a big, friendly and absolutely terrifying smile. "It's my little pal, Quinn. How are you doing, young man? Sleep well?"

Then he started walking slowly towards the truck, all the while staring straight at me. I even saw him lick his lips.

My mind started racing, grasping for an idea, any idea. I had to do something. My fear was so overwhelming I almost wet my pants. But I didn't. Instead, I did the only thing I could think of. I put my hand in my pocket and took out Sean's knife. I carefully held it below the sight line of the window and opened the blade, waiting, watching as Ronny came toward me, his smile confident. Honestly? I have to say, holding the knife didn't help all that much. I had no idea what I was going to do with it.

And that creep took his time coming for me that was for sure, one step after another, slow and steady, all the while my heart pounded in my chest like a kettle drum. And with every step he took towards me my fear grew and grew until my mind nearly exploded with terror. But it didn't, although I almost wish it had, because instead I was left with watching him while my brain whirled out of control, knowing that if I didn't do something quick there was no doubt that this guy, who had once been so nice and kind to me, was now going to do something bad to me.

As he walked he kind of sauntered, swinging his hips a

little, which freaked me out even more. He took a length of thin rope out of his back pocket and dangled it from his right hand, twirling it in a circle. With his left hand he raised it a little and started moving it back and forth like he was waving at me.

It took him maybe half a minute in total to cross towards me. Both the shortest and longest half minute of my life, and as he got closer, my fear turned to panic. I knew for sure I was going to die. When he was a few steps from the truck he started beckoning to me with his index finger like that witch in The Wizard of Oz. *I'm coming to get you.* God, I couldn't help it and I started shaking all over again.

When he reached the truck he put his right hand on the handle, rope dangling from it while he paused waiting, toying with me I guess, looking at me to see how'd I react. We were less than three feet apart; my only protection was the door of the truck, but with the window down that wasn't much. I took a deep breath to try to quit shaking without much success. He was so much bigger than me and he acted so confidently, like he could do anything he wanted to me which he for certain would. My eyes welled up and I fought back tears as I tried to get myself ready.

"Here I come, Quinn," he said, smiling with those brown teeth. "I'm glad you finally woke up."

With his right hand he pushed in the latch, opened the door wide and held it there. He suddenly seemed to grow taller right before my eyes, growing until he was gazing down upon me, looking me over while I crouched and cowered as he silently tormented me with eyes that now started to look like some sort of weird, slimy reptile's. I tried not to faint dead away with the worst fear I'd ever felt in my whole life. I knew he was going to rape and brutalize me and then he'd kill me.

Holding the door open he put his left hand out towards

me, reaching for me, but I wasn't going to wait. I had kept the knife in my right hand hidden behind me and I didn't hesitate. I fought through my fear as adrenalin took over. I screamed as loud as I could as I lunged out at him, stabbing out at his hand with my knife. I might have been small, but I was quick and I must have startled him because he moved at just that same moment I lunged. I missed his hand but that was okay because I slashed that razor sharp blade right across his forearm instead. Deep.

He stopped, startled, and looked at the cut. So did I. For an instant nothing happened and I remember thinking, *Oh, my God, I'm in for it now. What did I do wrong? Why wasn't he bleeding?* But then the blood came. In torrents, flowing out of the gash, running out of his arm, covering it like he'd dipped it in a bucket of red paint. Big drops started falling to the ground before they were followed by a river of blood.

Ronny screamed in shock and pain and fell back against the wide open door of the truck as he tried to stop the flow of blood with his right hand. He didn't have any success. His knees sagged a little and he looked at me with disbelief as he tried to collect himself. But only for a moment. Then his eyes pierced me with an anger and hatred so deep I almost froze again. But I didn't.

In an instant I slid off the seat and hit the ground running. He tried to grab me but I was able to push his bloody arm away and he screamed again. I bolted to the back of the truck, around it and then ran like hell to the river. I slid down the embankment and jumped into the muddy water thinking for some reason how refreshingly cool it felt. Then I fought my way out to the middle where I started swimming and floating downstream with the current. Was Ronny yelling and screaming and running after me? I don't know. My world had closed in and all I

106

thought about was survival. But I'll tell you this, I never looked back. And I didn't know where I was going, either, but I didn't care. I was getting away and that's all that mattered.

It was many minutes later I realized I still had the knife gripped in my hand. I rolled to my back and floated, closed it and managed to stuff it in my front pocket, thinking that Sean would kill me if I lost it. Funny what can come to your mind sometimes. Anyway, once the knife was safely put away, swimming became a lot easier.

I stayed in that river for as long as I could, my fear that Ronny was going to catch me becoming less and less the further I dogpaddled and swam. But I was still frightened and might even have floated in that muddy water all the way across the state of Minnesota to St. Paul if a farmer hadn't been tending to some cattle on the shore and seen me, called to me, and waded out into the water to drag me to safety. I realized then that I was close to being drowned, my thoughts of Ronny and what he might do if he caught me the only thing that was keeping me going – keeping me afloat so to speak. The farmer was old, strong, and kind enough to bring me up to his farmhouse; in fact he carried me most of the way in his arms. It was a big two story white home with a wide porch – just like you see sometimes on the television.

He brought me through the back door, right into the kitchen and set me down on a rug by the door, saying, "Greta, look at what I found."

Whether he was making a joke or not I didn't know, but his wife, who was stirring something on the stove, took one look and didn't hesitate but ran straight to me, smacked at her husband with her wooden spoon and told him to get some towels, which he did. She took over, helping me to the kitchen table where she sat me down, knelt on the floor, began drying me off and fussing over me which, I have to admit, even to this day the memory of still makes me feel really good.

The farmer looked on, his eyes topped by white eyebrows that I swear stuck half way up his forehead, giving me the once over while his wife worked on pampering me.

At one point she looked over her shoulder and said, "For pity's sake, Clive, don't just stand there dripping on the rug, get a towel and dry yourself off. I'm sure not going to do it for you." And he did.

When he was finished he took a pipe out of his overalls, filled it with tobacco and lit it before asking, "Your name wouldn't be Quinn by any chance?"

What the...? How'd he know? "Uh. Yes sir, it is." I told him. Then I immediately got suspicious and frightened all over again. After what I'd been through, who wouldn't? "Why?" I looked towards the back door as I wondered if I'd stepped into another bad situation and I'd have to make a run for it. Again.

"Clive, quiet down and don't bother the boy," his wife told him. "Can't you see he's frightened enough."

She turned to me and smiled, reassuring me, "Don't let him scare you, young man. His bark is way worse than his bite." She looked past me towards the old farmer and I could almost see daggers coming out of her eyes.

Clive, I guess that's what his name was, shuffled his feet on the rug, shook his head and said, "Didn't mean anything by it." He sucked on his pipe some more and considerately blew the smoke outside through the screen door. By this time I got the feeling his wife pretty much ran the show in that household.

She made sure I was comfortable in my chair at the table, and after she'd dried me off she went and got a big quilt that she wrapped around me. It smelled clean and fresh, just like outdoors. Then she went to the refrigerator and took out a bottle of milk. "You're all over the news," she said, pouring me a big glass. "We've been listening on the radio. The police have been looking for you. We heard you'd been kidnapped."

She brought me the milk with a heaped plate of chocolate chip cookies and set them in front of me. Suddenly I was famished and I started eating them right away. They were the best cookies I'd ever tasted. Then, or since.

While I was eating, Greta stood next to me, watching over me with a concerned expression. She was a large woman with her grey hair pinned up on top of her head and she wore an apron over her dress. She knelt down and felt my forehead and it didn't bother me at all – her attention felt kind of nice. She had blue-green eyes that I especially noticed when she peered closely and asked softly, "Are you Ok, Quinn?" Her breath smelled sweet, like peppermint.

"Yes, Maam, I am," I told her, swallowing after finishing off my third or fourth cookie. "I'm fine. I really am." And for the first time since I'd run from the truck I truly believed I was and, I have to say, with the relief I suddenly felt, my eyes filled with tears and I almost started to cry.

She pulled me to her bosom and hugged me tight.

Well, I never...And the tears starting running. She held me tighter and I could have stayed there forever.

When I was all cried out she released me, like she'd had a sudden thought, and turned to her husband. "Lordy, Lordy, Clive," she exclaimed. "What in heaven's name's the matter with you? What are you waiting for? Get on the phone right now and call Sheriff Nelson. Quick. Tell him we've got that boy they're looking for. Tell whoever answers that he's okay and that he's sitting right here in our kitchen."

Clive, whom I got the impression wasn't the fastest man alive, moved pretty darn quick under his wife's command and made the call.

That night I spent in the hospital in Ortonville. The next night I was home and I'll tell you this, after all I'd been through, even seeing Sean felt pretty good.

The morning I got home after Dad and Sexy Sal had gone to work, Sean and I were alone in the house for the first time since I'd been back. Everybody wanted me to rest, so my brother had to sleep in the living room on the couch which I don't think he minded too much because he could be close to his precious PlayStation. I'd given his knife back to him that evening and received nothing in return but a menacing scowl.

That morning he came into the bedroom. I immediately got nervous, my stomach tying itself all up in knots.

"So you stole my knife, huh?" he asked, sitting down on my bed and moving close.

I didn't answer right away. If I denied it, he might find out Lea took it and gave it to me and I didn't want her to get into trouble. If I admitted it, well then...my imagination took over leaving me with nothing but an unhappy ending. But hell, I'd had to deal with Ronny and I got through that all right. I figured I could take on anything – even whatever Sean had to dish out.

I puffed up my chest a little. "Yeah, I did," I told him, trying to sound tough. "So what?"

I looked at him and he looked right back at me. Two days ago the next move would have been me trying to get away and probably not succeeding, suffering Sean's version of justice with him proceeding to pound me into a bruised and battered, bloody little pulp, then walking away with a self-satisfied smirk on his face.

Sean surprised me by doing nothing violent. Instead, he

put his hand on top of my covers on my leg, but not in a mean way. I only flinched a little.

"You don't have to lie for her," he said. "I know what happened with the knife. Lea told me."

"What?" I screamed. "Is she all right?"

I tried to get up, but he held me back. I pictured my sweet natured little sister submitting to his wrath and the image was more than I could bear. Then I had a thought. Wait a minute. I'd already seen her when I got home. She'd been perfectly fine. She'd even given me a big hug and everything before retreating to her room with her dolls for the rest of the evening.

"Relax, man, she's Ok," he smiled. I accepted that Lea really was unharmed, but now Sean was smiling at me, which was creepy in itself. He never smiled at me. What was up with that?

"Seriously, she's just fine." He sounded almost like he was trying to reassure me. Like he knew I cared about Lea and he didn't want me to have to worry about her. He was acting really weird.

And he was also confusing me. Big time. He was right about my sister, of course, she truly was okay, but his behaviour was so different from how he normally acted that I have to admit I was stunned. I looked at him like he was nuts and he must have seen the disbelief in my eyes because he waited for me to say something. But I didn't. I couldn't think of anything to say.

Maybe a minute went by before he continued, "I admit I was mad. Pissed off is more like it. I really was ready to kill you." I involuntarily shuddered. He appeared not to notice and continued, "But then you were gone and no one knew where you were and someone found your bike up on the highway and called Dad who got mad and worried and he called the cops and..." he stopped and shrugged his shoulders. "And everything else happened and I just sort of forgot that I was mad at you."

What the hell? Was this real life or had I stepped into a fantasy world where nothing bad ever happens and there's unlimited ice cream with hot dogs every night for dinner and a happy ending?

I was pondering the significance of such a world and finding it to my liking when I sensed a movement at the bedroom door. I pulled myself back to reality and looked. There was Lea, peeking around the doorframe. She was safe and unharmed and she looked great. She took a tentative step into the room. "Hi," she said, shyly.

"Lea," I grinned and almost shouted, "Come here." I patted the side of the bed as I moved over.

She smiled back, ran to me and hugged me so tightly that for a moment I wondered where she got the strength for such a little thing. It almost hurt. Almost. And it felt great.

Sean stayed and sat on the bed with us. Suddenly it came to me that it was the first time we three had been together in our room for I don't know how long. If ever. And without fighting or anything. Like a normal family. I have to say it felt pretty good.

We talked a lot. Sean couldn't hear my story enough, especially the knife part, and he had me tell it over and over again until I finally got tired. I had been through a lot and it was still catching up with me. Finally he stood up, telling me that Mr. Jorgenson from the hardware store had called the night before and offered him his job back. "Yeah, he told me that when he'd heard what you had gone through and what you had done to get away, he thought maybe there was something in me that he'd missed. What do you think he meant by that?"

I had my own idea that Mr. Jorgenson hadn't missed

anything, but I certainly wasn't going to tell Sean that so I said only, "Maybe he was just being nice."

Sean shrugged. "Maybe. Anyway, I'm going down there now." He glanced at the clock on the night stand by my bed. I followed his gaze. It read a few minutes after nine. "Shit. I'm late. I'm supposed to be there right at nine. See ya'."

I watched as he ran out of the room. Then I caught Lea's eye. We looked at each other for a moment before my little sister pointed to Sean's disappearing back, then pointed to her head with her finger and twirled it around like 'He's crazy' and rolled her eyes. I couldn't believe it. She was making fun of Sean and it was funny! I laughed out loud for the first time in ages. It was then that I had the thought that it was actually great to be back home.

You know what? They never found Ronny. When the sheriff came and picked me up at Greta and Clive's place, he talked to me on the way to the hospital. I was able to give them an idea where I had been and he immediately sent some deputies to search the area. The truck, the tent and the dog kennel were all still there and surprise, surprise, no camping gear. But Ronny was nowhere to be seen. They searched the river, sent out hundreds of police type bulletins, dragged the river, everything they could think of. They never found him. My fervent hope is that he followed me into the river, the current got him, he drowned and was eaten by some big ugly fish with dull teeth. It would have served him right.

Dad and Sexy Sal pretty much acted the same as ever to me after I came home and I don't really want to talk about them.

But Sean and I got along better with each other. A lot better. I think the job at the hardware store helped – made him feel older and more responsible maybe. Anyway, he didn't pick on me so much afterwards, only sometimes joking with me, pretending like he was going to hit me, but he never did. I guess he just started to grow up some.

Lea and I became closer. I couldn't then, and still can't now, ever thank her enough for giving me Sean's knife that day. But maybe I was able to in some small way. She got me to play dolls with her a lot the rest of the summer right up until when school started and I didn't really mind. She was fun to be with and she had a really good imagination, especially when it came to using her dolls to play a game she called Family. I never did understand why she never had a lot of friends. Well, any, actually. Maybe she just liked being by herself. But she was a sweet kid and I figured playing with her and being kind of a friend to her was the least I could do after what she'd done for me, even if it had been inadvertent (another word I learned about in school.) I'm positive I wouldn't have escaped without her help.

Next year in seventh grade in the fall my teacher, Mrs. Rademacher, had us studying *The Adventures of Huckleberry Finn.* Now there's a lot of fancy imagery and stuff in the book that I didn't understand, but there were some other things that I kind of got what she was saying. Like at one point she talked about how at the end Huck sort of is rescued from his life on the river, ends up living with his Aunt Sally and everything is fine for him. But he doesn't like being civilized and decides to light out for the west. One of the points she was trying to make was about how life sometimes works in mysterious ways and there's no accounting sometimes for why things happen the way they do. Huck was rescued and had the good fortune to have the easy life all laid out for him, good food, clean clothes, a roof over his head, someone to love and care for him, and he chose to give it all up.

114

Mrs. Rademacher looked at me when she talked to us about that, but didn't mention me or refer the class to my story from the summer before. But yeah, I think I got what she was saying. Sometimes life does work in mysterious ways.

By the way, Mrs. Rademacher was really nice to me that whole entire year.

And that knife. Later that first day I was home, Sean came in from working at the hardware store and sat down on the bed next to me and woke me up from a nap.

"Here," he said. He handed me his knife. "I've been thinking about it all day." Which was surprising to me. Sean thinking about something? Was I still dreaming? I actually pinched myself a little. No, I was wide awake. I'd never thought of Sean as much more than a bully. A thinker? I didn't think so. Maybe he was changing. I doubted it but I guess stranger things could happen.

He looked at me like he meant what he was saying, "Seriously, I want you to have this." He reached over, gently took my hand and put his cherished knife in it.

I was shocked. I watched him closely to see if he was kidding but he wasn't. He put his hand over mine and said, "Really. After all you went through; I want you to have this. You deserve it."

I took his knife and held in my hand. I opened the blade. The sheriff's department had wiped it down for traces of blood before they gave it back to him. They must have cleaned it too because it was gleaming. I looked at it and saw my image on the blade reflected back. I looked tired. Real tired. Then the image changed and I saw something else. For the briefest moment I thought I saw Ronny smiling at me with those ugly brown teeth of his. Grinning at me like I was all his and he could take me and do anything he wanted to me. It freaked me out. I might have screamed. I don't know. But I do know that I quickly closed the blade and handed the knife back. I swear it felt hot to my touch like maybe it was possessed or something. I knew one thing. I didn't want to touch it again. Or have anything to do with it again. Ever.

I tried to compose myself and told him, "That's Ok, Sean. But thanks. I think I've had it with knives for a while."

He looked at me for a moment or two before putting the knife in his pocket. "Ok. I think I get it."

Well, that made only one of us because I certainly didn't. In fact, I just let the matter drop, but sometimes still to this day an image of Ronny will appear in my mind. And when it does, it's scary. People tell me that it's normal for that to happen, especially after all I had gone through. But I have to say, others have been through a lot worse. A way lot worse, and for the rest of my life I always counted myself as among one of the lucky ones. I got away.

Now I'll tell you one last thing. In the summer, three years later Sean started driving a delivery truck for the company my dad worked for and I began working at the hardware store. Even though I was still small for my age, Mr. Jorgenson was happy to have me, saying, "Sean turned out to be a good worker, but I'll bet you'll be lots better." Well, Sean had changed and actually gotten to be a pretty good guy and I didn't want say anything against him so all I did was to tell Mr. Jorgenson that I'd do my best.

The first thing I did with my first paycheck was to take my money and go to the knife display case. I'd spent many long and enjoyable hours looking at the knives in there in those three years since Ronny, picturing myself having one of my very own. One like Sean's, except a little bigger. I knew exactly the knife I wanted and so I bought it, snapped open the blade a few times, getting the feel of it and the balance of it. It felt good. Finally, I closed it up, put it in my pocket, said goodbye to Mr. Jorgenson and went outside to get my bike and hurried home.

Lea was standing at the back door waiting for me. She ran outside, jumped on the back and we rode down to the park. We spent an enjoyable hour, swinging on the swings, playing on the merry-go-round, climbing on the jungle-gym and running up and down the slides, acting silly and goofing around. We had a fun time. She even laughed out loud a few times.

Before we came home we found some purple and white wildflowers that Lea liked so I cut a bouquet of them for her with my new knife. She carried them carefully in her hand all the way back to our house to put them in a small juice glass that she filled with water from the kitchen faucet. Then she took them to her room and set them on her window ledge.

"My dolls like them, Quinn," she told me. I was standing at her door watching, happy that she was happy. She looked at me and said, "So do I." And then she smiled and waved as I closed the door. Standing in the hall and listening, I heard her saying, "Come on now girls, let's play family."

I went into the kitchen, got an apple and sat on the back step to eat it. I used my knife to cut it up. It sliced really good. Tasted good, too. When I was finished, I cleaned off the blade on my jeans and put it in my pocket. It felt good to have it there.

After all these years I'm not sure if it helps or not, but I have to say that I like having my knife with me. It gives me a sense of security that I just can't explain. But when those images of Ronny appear and I start to freak out a little, I put my hand on my knife and they go away. I like knowing that I can do that – that I have some control. And it gives me a little sense that I might not be a victim after all. Or ever again. But, I carry it with me every day. Just in case.

And you know what? I never once thought about running away from home again.

Speckled Toad Beer

I hate to admit it, but I never knew that the inspiration for the character of Uncle Sam in the WWI recruitment poster was the artist himself. Apparently he'd dilly-dallied on doing the painting until it was almost too late, so he did the initial drawing based on his own reflection in the mirror. He liked what he saw and from that first draft he completed the work, adding the bushy eyebrows, craggy features and the pointed, somewhat threatening finger that to this day is still an iconic American symbol.

My wife and I had been watching a special on our local PBS station when the story behind the poster was explained. I liked what I was hearing and it gave me an idea. *Why not do the same thing, using myself as a model for the Speckle Toad Beer ad campaign I was working on?*

I floated my thought past Michelle. It didn't take her long to express her opinion. "You're nuts, Troy," she said, and popped a kernel of popcorn into her mouth from the bowl we'd been sharing to emphasize her point. "Absolutely and completely out of your mind," she added, grabbing a big handful to further solidify her opinion.

"Why? What's wrong? I think it's a great idea."

She let out a soft belch and looked me right in the eye. Michelle has taught third grade at the Orchard Lake elementary school for fifteen years. She's good at it; dare I say, even great. She has a firm but loving hand with the kids which makes her popular with both the students and their parents. She also tells it like it is and doesn't pussy foot around with the truth. "Who would really care to see an image of you on an advertisement for beer?" She held up her hand with her thumb and pointer finger forming a zero. "Seriously, Troy, my guess is no-one." She chuckled to herself and went back to the popcorn, figuring she'd made her point.

In her mind she probably did. But me? I'm a little slow on the uptake. I should have listened to her.

I'm in my mid-forties and have worked for nineteen years in the art department for Lavender Hill Design, a well-known upper Midwest firm specializing in creating advertisements focused on small businesses. We'd recently hit it big with the local craft beer industry and I've been one of the most successful designers. Maybe longevity and success had gone to my head, but I ignored my wife's advice and proceeded with my plan of using my own image in the ad campaign. In World War I it was Uncle Sam saying "I Want You." Now, for my ad, I was hoping to come up with something like 'Speckled Toad Beer is the beer for you,' with my face serving as the spokesperson.

I took some selfies and then used them to make preliminary sketches. Then I used my oil paints to create the perfect image. After a couple of weeks of work I had my character, 'The Face of Speckled Toad Beer' as I secretly called it, and was ready to present my creation to my design team at the end of the week.

My presentation was on that Friday. When I was finished, I can honestly say that I had never heard people laugh so hard.

That night I dragged myself home and plunked down on the couch, the same couch where a month earlier we'd watched that ill-fated PBS special.

"Bad day at the office dear?" Michelle asked, sitting next to me and handing me a gin and tonic.

"You might say," I said, gratefully sipping my drink.

She grinned. "I told you so. Want to tell me what happened?"

I did.

"The image I created used my enhanced selfie and a character I painted that was dressed in a coonskin cap and buckskins like that Davy Crockett character my dad used to watch back in the fifties. I thought it would be charming and homey. It was not a good move."

Michelle snuggled up next to me, took a sip from my drink and gave me a sympathetic, "Aw, poor boy." Then she unsuccessfully tried to hide a grin. "Tell me more." It didn't help that she was really enjoying this, but I guess in a way I deserved it.

"I began by putting the image of the Speckled Toad Beer character up on the screen in the front of the room. It was just my four person team and Kate Williams our supervisor. It took her about three seconds to break out in hysterics. When she caught her breath and quit laughing, she told me that an amphibian dressed up in buckskins wasn't going to cut it.

"It went downhill from there when the rest of my team joined in laughing. The rugged character I'd hoped to portray ended up looking like a deranged mountain man. I don't know which was worse; the fact that I'd blown the presentation, or that everyone thought my face looked like a toad." I sighed and leaned back on the couch. "The general consensus was that instead of selling beer it would more likely scare people away from buying it. Back, as they say, to the drawing board."

Michelle gave me a quick kiss, looked me in the eyes and said, "See, you should have listened. I really do know what I'm talking about, you know."

She was right. I don't know what I'd been thinking. "Yeah, I hear you. I guess I let my ego get in the way." I sighed and sipped my drink, starting to come to grips with the fact that I wasn't nearly as smart as I thought I was.

She picked up the remote. "You want to watch some television?" She started scanning the shows. Then she stopped and looked at me, joking, "We can risk it, right?

121

You're not going to let some show give you any more crazy ideas?"

I laughed. "Funny. No, I think I've learned my lesson. From now on I'll just stick with what I know, art and advertising."

"Good idea." It took her less than a second to agree.

She found a program she liked and we watched. It was filmed in England and had something to do with a baking contest. Interestingly, the contestants were vying to win, but they were also quite pleasant to each other. It was nice to see. Maybe they were on to something, and it gave me an idea. I wondered if maybe the ad could say something like, "Speckled Toad Beer, a beer that treats you kindly." It sounded good and had a nice ring to it.

I'll start working on a new ad campaign tomorrow. But this time I'll keep my face out of it.

Storm Clouds

A small group of Minnesota's criminally insane are housed in a grey, nondescript building on the outskirts of the town of Epps in the northwestern part of the state. It's flatland soybean and corn fields up there, and I'm getting to know the area pretty well. It makes sense. I've been coming here every month for the last thirty-three months. It's where my son Tim has been sentenced to spend the rest of his life. I'm told he's never going to leave. Just imagining what he's going through inside those walls causes the storm clouds to start to build in my brain. I close my eyes and do my mental exercises to get myself under control. If those clouds build and explode into lightning who knows what'll happen? Someone could get hurt, that's for sure. They have in the past, and it hasn't been pretty. Thankfully, I'm successful. The anger settles and recedes. I feel myself calming down.

I've had a problem controlling my temper my entire life. It started when I was young. If I didn't get my way, man, I tell you, there'd be hell to pay. I used to get into a lot of fights. A few times I even ended up in the hospital. And that all happened before I got out of grade school.

Fortunately, over time I was able to change. What happened? I wish I could say that I had a simple answer or a magic formula, but it really just came down to wanting to do more with my life than spend it being a pugilistic jerk who settled his arguments with his fists. My father left home when I was nine, my mom needed me to help her raise my two younger brothers, so one thing led to another and I just figured out how to control my temper, my anger, my rage. I learned not to let those storm clouds get the better of me. Apparently, I failed to teach my son the same thing.

I pulled into the tiny parking lot of the facility and walked to the front entrance. The building is a former grade school that underwent extensive renovation twenty years ago. It's actually called the Marshall County Prison. My son is housed with a few other inmates in one wing called the Behavioural Study Unit. A team of doctors are analysing him to see if they can determine why he did what he did. So far they have no answers.

I shouldered my backpack and headed for the front entrance. After going through two security checkpoints I'm taken to the nurses' office where I meet with Connie Greyeagle. She filled me in on the medications they are giving Tim.

Nearly three years ago, my son suddenly snapped. He stole a rifle from a neighbour and went on a rampage, killing seven people. He was twenty years old at the time. To make a long story short, the doctors think that there was something manifesting itself in his brain that caused him to do what he did. He's now a risk to society. Medication is one way they are treating him for his violent behaviour and mood swings. Connie and I talked awhile and then she ushered me to Anderson Gingsrude's office, the psychiatrist in charge of my son.

"Hi, Anders," I greet him and we shake hands. "How's Tim doing?"

"As well as can be expected."

The response he gives me is the same every time we meet, vague enough to give me hope without telling me anything concrete. That's fine with me. At this stage of the game, hope goes a long way. It's certainly better than nothing. I'll take it.

Anders is a good guy. Fifty years ago he might have been a cigarette smoking overweight control freak who could not have cared less about the patients under his supervision. But that kind of attitude is not acceptable these days. He has the lean body of a marathoner (which he is), and a helpful manner. He fills me in on how Tim is doing, primarily about the team from the University of Minnesota who have developed a rigorous set of tests on genetics and what part my genes could have played in influencing Tim's violent outburst. Let me tell you, knowing I might have had a role to play biologically in Tim's killing spree is sobering. It's something I'm having to learn to deal with and probably will be for the rest of my life. It's not easy, but I'm doing my best.

We talked for a while and then he walked with me to the door outside my son's room, an eight by ten space made of twelve inch thick concrete.

"Good bye, Sam," he tells me, shaking my hand and giving me a sympathetic look. "Thanks for coming." He puts his other hand over our two clasped ones. "Take care."

Like I said, he's a nice guy.

This end of the wing is eerily silent. Depressing is putting it mildly. Anders unlocked the door before he left, so I go inside pull up a chair and sit down. Tim's taller than me by three inches and thinner by fifty pounds. They keep his head shaved due to the tests they run on him, but his eyebrows are still bushy brown and his eyes are the same dark amber they've been since he was two years old.

"Hi, son," I say. I watch him carefully for any signs that he recognizes me. There are none. He doesn't look at me. Or answer me. Or even acknowledge me. Nothing. He sits passively in a recliner and stares into space. Dr Gingsrude tells me it's the drugs that do it; they make my once outgoing and effervescent son almost catatonic.

"It's better this way," the doctor has told me. "He's easier to manage."

His statement is not easy to accept, but my son is a cold blooded killer who took the lives of seven innocent people. I'm trying to accept the fact that, compared to being a violent murderer, Tim being in a catatonic state is better. It is better, right? I don't know. All I know is that he is my son and I still love him.

"Tim, I've got something for you," I tell him and right then and there begins a one-sided conversation that will last for the next four hours, the amount of time I am allowed to spend with my boy. From my back pack I take out a floral arrangement my wife Anne has put together. This time it's a pretty bouquet of yellow geraniums. I set them in the plastic vase I've brought with me (glass is not allowed) and fill it with a bottle of water from my pack. I set the vase and flowers on the night stand next to his bed.

Next I take out a tin of cookies Jenny my daughter and Tim's younger sister made for him. This visit it's chocolate chip, a favourite of his from a time long ago. I offer them to him, but, again, no response, so I set them aside. I take out an iPod and plug it into a small boom box I always bring. I turn it on. I like to play the music Tim used to listen to growing up. He doesn't acknowledge he hears anything.

Finally I take out the book I've brought along and settle in to read to him. It's number three in a series by a Minnesota author set in the fictional town of Aurora, about a hundred miles east of where we are right now.

All the time I've been with him Tim hasn't responded to one thing I've said or done, but that's okay. He never does, and I'm used to it. I try not to let the sadness I feel get to me. There'll be time later for that. Right now it's good to be with my son. I settle back and begin reading out loud.

In no time at all, it seems, there's a knock on the door. It's an orderly telling me my visit is over. "I've got to go, Tim," I tell him. "I'll be back next month." I stand up and kiss his forehead. I gather up my book and the other things I brought, put them in my backpack and quietly close his door. I walk down the hall to the nurses' station where I leave the cookies and flowers with Connie. He's not allowed to have anything in his room other than the bed, night stand and the two chairs.

"Good bye," I say to Connie. "See you next month."

"Good bye, Sam," she says. "Good to see you. He's the only one around here who gets a visitor."

I shrug my shoulders. What can you say? He's my son and I'll never stop coming. I leave without saying anything.

There's a truck stop on the interstate a mile outside Epps and that's where I'm headed. I'm wiped out and need some caffeine. Plus, I'm low on gas. I pull up to the pump and start to fill up my little Ford Fiesta. A car full of kids pulls in on the other side and one of them gets out and starts filling the tank. A few minutes go by. I'm thinking about Tim and planning my next visit when a commotion startles me back to the present.

An attendant is running out of the station, yelling, "Hey you guys, stop! You didn't pay for your gas."

"Screw you, pal!" the kid who was at the pump yells back.

He's starting to get in his car when I step across the island and grab him and jam him up against a concrete support structure. He pushes back, slugs me in the chest and my vision explodes into bright light. Violent storms clouds build exponentially in my brain, billowing and turning black as night.

I react quickly and grab the kid with both hands tightly by the front of his shirt. "Hey, there, pal," I say, giving him a shake and looking straight into his eyes. "It looks like you owe this gentleman here some money. Give it to him!" I shake him, again. Hard. I can see his eyes roll back in his head. It is at this point, in the past, things could have gotten ugly. I could have gone berserk and maybe even beaten the kid to a pulp. Hurt him bad.

127

But not now. Now, I get control of myself, grit my teeth and give him a command. "Didn't you hear me? I said, give him his money." I am right in his face and emphasize, "Now."

I feel his hot breath on my face. It smells like fear. He must have sensed something in me. Something frightening. I know what he's feeling. He's feeling my rage, barely under control. Barely. I'm doing my best to keep it there.

So, he does the smart thing. He pays the attendant and even apologizes to the young man. And to me. "You did a good thing by paying," I tell the kid after things have settled down. "Make sure you don't forget next time."

He blinks and gives me a nod. Then, without a word, he gets in the car and he and his friends slowly drive away.

Later, driving home, I think about my son and the treatment he's receiving for his violent behaviour. I think about how the doctors are studying his genes and my genes to see if there's any kind of correlation; to see if there's something genetic that made him do what he did. They hope that the knowledge will help form a foundation for helping others in the future.

My fingers are crossed that they'll be successful. It never is far from my mind, knowing that I could have had a role to play in Tim turning out the way he did. The truth? I probably did. I know that. It makes perfect sense. That's why I see my son as often as I can. I'm his dad, and I owe him that much. Besides, it's the least I can do. We have a lot in common. Half of him is me, and, it's not too far of a stretch for me to realize the awful truth. It could easily have been me sitting in there.

The Mosquito

My arms were propped on my wheelchair. My wife Karen had rolled me onto the back patio saying, "It's a beautiful June day, Jake. Time for some sunshine. You're starting to look a little pale." She smiled at me, a little joke between us since I don't get outside like I used to.

I'd always loved being in the out of doors and still do, despite the fact that being outside contributed to the state I'm in now; confined to a wheelchair for the rest of my life. I'd been riding my bicycle through a forest on the Lucy Line Trail a few miles from our home when a hundred feet in front of me a barred owl dropped down out of a tree. The big raptor took a few strong wing beats and then glided right toward me. Mesmerized, I watched him coast past on my right, not ten feet away.

I turned to watch, lost control of my bike, veered over the side of the trail and careened down a deep ravine. I smashed my head into a tree and severed my spine. I will never walk again. Ever. I can't even move my arms. Nothing. I can't even talk. The only thing I can do is blink my eyes, which makes it hard to express myself, but I'm learning. It's been one year, one month and thirteen days since the accident. I hope I'm trying to make the best of things, and I think I am. After all, I don't have much choice, do I?

But some things really get to me. I can no longer hug Karen, or my kids, or my grandchildren. That loss of physical contact is hard, never being able to touch or feel a loved one. Man, I miss it. And don't get me started on my inability to talk. Even though I was never the most verbose person in the room, not being able to communicate is frustrating, sometimes downright irritating. Especially now. Now that a mosquito has landed on the back of my hand on a throbbing, exposed, blue vein. I watch as it fills its tiny body with my blood. It's not fun. I want to call out to Karen to come and at least brush it away, but I can't. Of course, I can't feel anything, but it's the principle of the thing that matters here. I watch as the unwelcome insect swells larger and larger, blowing up like a living balloon, its transparent body turning bright red, engorged with my blood.

Karen, where are you? Please, I need you. You said you'd be right back.

I watch the mosquito and use all my will power to move my hand. Nothing happens and my frustration begins building. I know Karen's got other things to do, but, damn. It's hard to watch this thing filling itself calmly, unafraid of any repercussions. Even harder to ignore it.

Shit. I can't stand this. I hate not being able to do anything for myself. I can't even tell my loved ones how much I cherish them and appreciate them and all they do for me. All I can do is sit here and watch that damn mosquito have its way with me.

After what seems like an hour, I hear Karen's happy voice calling from behind me, "Jake, I'm back. I just went for some ice tea. I thought a little treat would taste refreshing." She'd been gone maybe a minute.

Out of the corner of my eye, I watch as she moves into view. She sets the two glasses down on the table next to me. Mine has a straw. Then she reacts as she sees the mosquito. "Oh, my god." Quickly, her hand darts out and she smacks it, blood spurting, leaving a satisfying smear. "Got it," she says and smiles happily. "Glad I got back in time." Then she wets a napkin with her tongue and cleans away the blood from the back of my hand.

If I could shed a tear of happiness right now, I would. Not just that she killed that mosquito, but that she was here to do it. My wife of over thirty years, she tells me she will never leave me. My God, how fortunate am I?

She carefully picks up my glass and brings it to me, guiding the straw to my lips. Our eyes make contact and I try to express my deep love for her. I try my best.

"Let's have our tea," she says.

Yes, let's, my love. Let's have our tea, I wish I could say.

Slowing Down

"Tommy, can we rest up ahead?" Mom gasped holding her hand to her chest. "This old heart..." The words trailed off.

She was in the final stage of congestive heart failure and it was a real bitch. "Sure, Mom," I said gently. "Here, take my hand."

With no argument she put her hand in mine, and we made our way to the bench fifteen feet away. It took five minutes.

As we walked I gazed down at my mother, a tiny, bird of a woman, thin as a rail, her formally auburn hair now snow white. "I'm keeping it natural," she told me once, "the way it was meant to be."

Mom was like that, independent. She became a single mother at thirty-one to four children (I was the oldest) after dad left home without a word. That was fifty-three years ago. To help make ends meet she worked part time as a cashier in a local grocery store, then later, after we'd grown, she'd become a teaching assistant helping out at the local grade school. She was a friend to many and beloved by all.

Now this. These slow steps towards the end of her full life.

We sat down and looked out over the wetlands behind the senior living complex she'd called home for the last seven years. Suddenly, excited, she pointed. "Tommy, look, a family of ducks. What are they? Mallards?"

"Yes they are, Mom. Cute, aren't they?"

She smiled. "Little puff ball babies. They're so sweet."

We watched the mother and five ducklings in silence. I listened to Mom's breathing as it finally slowed down, becoming less laboured. She still held my hand. I squeezed it and said, "Mom, what about it? Should we think about a wheel chair for you? It would make it easier for us to be out and about."

"I don't know. I'm not sure."

I nudged her gently. "How long did it take us to get down to this bench?" I asked, trying to make a point.

Mom was no dummy. "Don't get smart with me, young man," she said, barking a phase she used with me quite a lot when I was growing up.

I smiled. "Well, the point is, it took us forty-five minutes. Last year we could make this walk in ten."

She patted my hand, her tone softened. "I know, but I just don't know if I'm ready to make that step." She paused, then added, "No pun intended."

I laughed. She had always had a good sense of humour.

We stayed on the bench for most of the afternoon. We watched the mother with her ducklings and, later, we even saw a great white egret land nearby. I'll always remember that day.

Three months later she passed away in her sleep. We never did get that wheelchair; we just slowed our walks down and didn't go very far. And when she got tired, I carried her. I think she enjoyed it. I know I did. She was my mom. It was the least I could do.

Flying

Dad thought it'd be a good idea to bring us along.

"You boys will like it. Mr. and Mrs. Bailey have three girls about the same age as you."

Jerry and I looked at each other, silently agreeing between us that it would be fun, but of course, we couldn't let our parents know that.

I complained, "Aw, no way. I don't want to go. Jerry and I were going to go to the creek and hunt carp with our bow and arrows."

Dad's eyes turned steely under thick black eyebrows. He gave us each a look only he was capable of. "I don't care. You're both coming with your mom and me. No arguments." Then he turned to our little brother, Brian, pointed a long index finger at him and said, "You, too."

So we went.

Mr. and Mrs. Bailey lived ten miles south of us on a bluff overlooking the Minnesota River. For our parents, the view was spectacular. For me and Jerry, well, all we carried about were the girls. Especially me. I was thirteen that summer with wild hormones running out of control. A lot of times I had no idea what was going on with me, often wondering, *Who's this guy that's taken over my body? What has he done with the mild mannered kid I used to be? Why did he make me do some of the things I did and fill my brain all those crazy thoughts?* I had no clue, but I was doing my best to hang on for the crazy ride.

Jerry, two years younger, was not only my brother, but also a pretty good friend. We did a lot of stuff together, so if I wanted to check out the Bailey's daughters he'd be right on board. Younger brother Brian? Well, at seven years old, he was hardly a passing thought. Really, who cared about him, anyway?

After a half hour on the road, Dad pulled into the driveway of the Bailey's sprawling rambler. I'd never in my life seen a house so big and long and, well, rambling. It went on forever. Mr. Bailey, like Dad, was an airline pilot. But he must have been better at his job than my father or something because it was obvious the guy was wealthy. He had three cars parked in the huge garage, one of them a shining dark green Jaguar. The huge front yard was shady, lush and green, almost like a jungle, and landscaped with shrubs and trees and gardens outlined with big, smooth, rounded stones. There was even a fountain in the middle of a pool in a rock garden with a beguiling naked lady shooting a ten foot stream of water out of her mouth. It was like being in another world.

Mr Bailey came out to greet us as we were getting out of our old Chevrolet station wagon. "Hey there, Fred," he grinned, shaking hands with my dad. "Mary, nice to see you." He gave my mom a brief hug and peck on the cheek. Then he turned to us. "And you must be Fred's boys," he exclaimed, pasting that fake smile on his face every parent is so good at. "How are you doing, young fellas?"

We had been raised to be polite so we all dutifully smiled and shook his proffered hand. He then turned and yelled at the top of his voice, "Girls! Get out here! The boys have arrived!"

Jesus, could this be any more embarrassing? I could feel my face turning beet red. I was at an age where parents drawing attention to me was the last thing I wanted. *Just shut up, Mr. Bailey, please, just shut up.*

Right then the girls appeared, strutting out through a door at the back of the garage like they were on a fashion runway. Three of them. Each pretty close to the age of Jerry, Brian and me, but that's where any similarity ended, and ended fast. We were obviously in a different league out here on the Minnesota River than back home in Minneapolis.

It was summer time. I was dressed in pressed Bermuda shorts and a white J Crew short sleeved shirt. On my feet were topsiders with no socks. It was a very preppy look, one encouraged by my dad and one I went along with just to keep peace in the family. Also, and this is more to the point, it was the style of clothes my friends wore, with only the slightest room for any variation, pattern on the Bermudas and colour of shirt being the only two worth mentioning.

Mr. Bailey said, "Boys, these are my daughters, Sharon, Kate and Jackie. Girls, say hello to Mr. Jacobson's boys."

Oh, my God. I'd never expected anything like his three girls, especially the oldest, Sharon. She was probably close to my thirteen years, except that she looked like she was twenty. She wore a dark purple halter top falling off one shoulder and the shortest, tightest, cut-off blue jeans I'd ever seen. Her auburn hair was tinged with red highlights and it fell in long ringlets over her bare suntanned shoulders. Her eyes were big and brown and covered in dark makeup, her lips painted deep lavender. Around her neck she wore a choker necklace on a chain with a peace symbol on it. A musky scent emanated from her that was strangely attractive. (I found out a few years later it was patchouli oil.) She had a henna hummingbird tattooed on one shoulder and a red heart with an arrow through it on the other. I was speechless.

She confidently walked right up to me and said, "So, like, hi. What was your name again?"

My mouth was so dry, I could barely stammer, "John." Which ended up coming out as a squeak because, I swear to god, my voice broke right then and there. I felt my face turn a deeper shade of red, if that were possible, maybe crimson.

136

She stood not more than two feet away and she gave me a long, slow, once over. I'm sure I quit breathing while she scrutinized me. After what seemed like forever but was probably only about five seconds, she smirked, took a step back, smacked the gum she was chewing, turned to her father and said, "I can't stay. Randy's picking me up in a few minutes." Then she turned on her heel and sauntered back through the garage, her two sisters trailing behind.

Well, I never.

I was mesmerized. I couldn't help it, my eyes were glued to her, my heart was running away with me. Perspiration beaded up on my forehead. I think I fell in love for the first time in my life right then and there. Too bad for me. The feeling was definitely not reciprocated. I never saw her again. But maybe seeing Sharon and knowing that I was out of my league out there on the Minnesota River at the home of my Dad's rich friend, led me to do what I did later that day. I don't know. But what I did was sure out of character for me that was for sure.

After Sharon left with Randy, her sisters took off down the road to hang out with some of their girl friends. We certainly weren't invited. That left Jerry, Brian and me to our own devices. The parents went inside to have drinks.

"You boys go outside and play," Mr. Bailey said. "Just watch out for the backyard," he laughed. "It's very steep, and it's a real bitch."

"Okay, thanks for the warning." I waved and immediately led Jerry and Brian out of the front door and around to the backyard. Why not? 'It's steep and it's a bitch,' rang in my ear. Sounded like fun to me.

The Bailey's home had been built at the top of a high ridge that ran a couple of hundred feet above the Minnesota River Valley. It offered spectacular views: the river, forests, swamps, backwaters, the whole nine yards. The back slope was in the process of being landscaped and terraced from the top of the ridge all the way down to the valley floor. The first terrace was in place. The second yet to be completed. We goofed around on the first terrace for about a minute. It was boring. Then we slid down to the top of the second terrace and peered over the edge. It was cut away like a cliff and there was a sloping drop-off for one hundred feet to the bottom, all of it made up of sand and debris from the work done on the house and the rest of the backyard.

"Cool," Jerry said in awe, standing at the edge.

"No kidding," I replied, looking out into the tops of the trees in the dense woods below. I picked up a fist sized stone. "Let's throw some rocks."

So we pitched rocks over the edge, the bigger the better, and watched them roll all the way to the bottom. It was fun, a nice diversion, and helped me to pretty much forget about the auburn-haired Sharon.

After fifteen minutes Jerry and I had worked up a sweat, so we took a break from our rock throwing to sit down to catch to our breath. Brian wasn't tired. He picked up some small pebbles and began to carefully toss them over. I watched him, my skinny little brother, seven years old, so sweet and innocent. Almost loveable. Then I had an idea.

"Hey, Brian," I said, "I've got a really good idea. We're up so high. How about if Jerry and I throw you over the edge of the cliff? It'd be fun, almost like flying."

I couldn't believe that those words had actually come out of my mouth. I knew it'd be dangerous, tossing him off a cliff. What was I thinking? I was the oldest and supposed to be in charge for Pete's sake. I was about to laugh it off and make a joke of it when Brian said, without hesitation, "Sure. If you think it'll be okay."

The trust of a younger brother. What an amazing thing,

is what I thought to myself. To him I said, "Sure. No sweat. You'll be fine." I had no idea what I was talking about.

Jerry and I stood up and made ourselves ready. I had Brian lie down on his back next to the edge of the cliff. I grabbed his hands, Jerry grabbed his feet. We lifted him up and swung him back and forth a few times to get the feel of him. He was very light. It was like swinging a teddy bear. We began to swing him over the edge, out into space. I counted off, "One...Two..."

In the middle of the third swing, Brian said, "You sure I'll be okay?"

I said, "Absolutely. No problem." And at the end of that swing I said to Jerry, "Three. Let him go."

And we did.

My God, to this day, I'll never forget how he flew out of our hands, Brian's small body framed against the blue sky as it hung suspended in space. For a poetic instant anyway. Then he dropped like a bag of wet cement and fell out of sight. Amazingly, he never screamed, flying through the air like he did. I certainly would have. He did, however, land with a soft thud thirty feet below us. Jerry and I both peered over the edge. The slope was gentle enough and the sand soft enough that the landing wasn't too hard. Fortunately, he wasn't injured. He did, however, roll all the way to the bottom of the ravine, a hundred feet below.

I was aghast at what I'd done. My little brother had trusted me and here I'd gone ahead and thrown him off a cliff. What an idiotic thing to do. He could have been killed. I jumped off the edge and scurried down the sandy incline as fast as I could, Jerry following behind. I needed to make sure Brain was all right. Fortunately, he was. In fact, he even laughed a little as we cleaned the sand off him. But he did make a point of telling me he didn't want to do it again. Well, no kidding.

Did tossing my little brother off that cliff have anything to do with my conflicted feelings about Sharon? I don't know. Maybe. I was definitely caught in the world between being a kid and being an adult, with the obvious conclusion that I really didn't fit into either. At least not on that particular day.

After we dusted Brian off, we three brothers climbed back to the top of the terrace and threw some more rocks over the edge. As we did, I felt that something had changed between Brian and me. The fact that he had trusted me...I don't know. It was touching, really. The fact that I betrayed that trust, well, that was something that made me feel like a jerk. I vowed to try to be a better brother to him. In the years to come, I wasn't always successful, but at least I tried. One thing was for sure, though, on that day I began to feel a little closer to him. He didn't seem like an annoying little kid anymore. We even threw a couple of big rocks together that required both of us to lift them. It was fun.

We stayed on the back terrace until Dad yelled at us to get ready to go home. We climbed back up to the sprawling house, got in the car and left. We never saw Mr. Bailey or his daughters ever again. That was probably a good thing.

Jerry, Brian and I have stayed close and Brian, to his credit, has never held a grudge against me and Jerry. At least that's what he says. I admire him for that because if the roles were reversed I certainly would have. In fact, he's always quick to point out, when we tell the story, that he was only a little scared. Mostly, though, he remembers that it really did feel like flying, falling through space like he did on that summer day so many years ago.

He also tells me he was glad that it happened. I don't know if I really believe him or not, but, if it's true, maybe it's one reason why he became a pilot later in life and flew airplanes for a living, just like our Dad. Oh, and his whole life he's also only lived in houses that have a flat backyard. No terraces for him. Not ever again. I can't say I blame him at all.

Sharpening the Blade

Last weekend Joyce bought a vintage push lawnmower at a garage sale. I used to use one like it as a kid mowing my parent's small yard in Minneapolis, so today I was fixing it up, on a bit of a nostalgia trip. I was back by the garage taking the wheel off when a movement out near the street caught my eye. I looked up just as my ten year old son Kyle called, "Hey, Dad. Check this out!"

I watched as he raced up our gravel driveway on his trek dirt bike pedalling at break neck speed for all he was worth. I didn't have any time to react and get worried before he threw the bike into a long two wheel slide and skidded to a stop less than three feet from me, spewing sand and grit all over the place. He hopped off and grinned. "How about that? Me and Nick have been practicing all morning."

Two years ago, before I came down with my illness, I'd have admonished him for riding so recklessly by saying, "You'd better watch yourself, you might fall and get hurt." I'd have taken him by the shoulder, looked him in the eye and reminded him that that's how accidents were caused. I probably would have added, "You might even get yourself killed," just to make my point.

But today I didn't do or say any of those things. At this stage of the game, it was just good to see him having fun. "Nice slide," I said, meaning it. "Looks like you and your buddy spent your time wisely."

That was another thing. Earlier in the summer, Kyle and Nick had ridden their bikes down to spend the afternoon at Orchard Lake, located only a half a mile from us. Late in the afternoon they were swimming from the beach out to the floating raft which was about a hundred and fifty feet from shore. A speed boat driven by a drunken twenty year old came roaring in from across the lake and swung too close to the swimming area, narrowly missing both boys. Fortunately, they hadn't been injured but it scared them half to death and, consequently, put them off swimming for the foreseeable future. I didn't blame them.

Kyle knelt by my side and took in the scene of me on the ground in front of the garage, fooling around with what to most people would look like a useless piece of junk. He asked, looking slightly perplexed, "What are you doing Dad? I thought we already had a lawn mower. You know, the one I use."

"We still do. That nice three horsepower Toro. But your mom got this at a yard sale and I thought I'd fix it up." I glance up quickly. Kyle hasn't hit his growth spurt yet and is as skinny as a whip. He has a mop of brown hair that he wears like the Beatles did when they first started out. He's quick to smile, has wide, deep brown, eyes and long eye lashes. Joyce says that one day he'll be a lady killer. Maybe, but I'm not really thinking about that right now. I'm happy with him just the way he is, a fun loving kid who'll be going into sixth grade next fall. "Want to help?" I ask.

He turns serious. "Sure."

"All right. Great. I've already taken the wheel off. Next step is to get the mower off the ground a few inches. You can lift it for me. We'll set the axel on this piece of wood."

Kyle follows my instructions to the letter. He's a great kid and likes to learn new things. He's hardly any trouble at all. I'm lucky.

The four slightly curved blades are attached to the axel. With the mower off the ground, the blades can spin freely. "What's next?" he asks.

I point. "Next we sharpen this bad boy." I open up a jar of sharpening compound and say, making a sly gesture, "This is the fun part." I dab some of the black gunk on my finger and rub it along the edge of one of the blades. It has

143

the consistency of peanut butter. I hand Kyle the jar. "Here, you do it, too."

"Oh boy," he grins enthusiastically and grabs a glob.

For the next minute we dutifully smear the granular sharpening compound along the blades. When we're done I insert a metal crank onto the end of the axel. "Okay, use this. Turn the wheel counter clockwise. The blades sharpen themselves against the bottom runner."

He carefully takes hold of the handle and begins to turn it. "Like this?" We both grimace as the blades make a grating, grinding noise, metal on metal.

"Yep. Keep it up. You're doing great," I say, speaking louder to make my voice heard above the racket.

He grins and cranks the handle faster. "This is fun."

In a minute the metal grinding becomes less and less until the assembly begins to spin freely indicating that the blades are completely sharpened. I smile thinking how great it is to be with my son. I wouldn't trade times like these for anything.

Next, I show Kyle how to clean the rest of the mower with light motor oil and WD-40. Finally, we put the wheel back on and I show him how to use a crescent wrench to tighten it, which he does. Then, just like that, our work is complete.

"Good job," I tell him.

Kyle stands up and brushes driveway dirt off his jeans. "Now what?"

"Well, if you want, you can take it for a spin."

Kyle looks at me questioningly. "What do you mean?"

"You know. Cut the grass."

"You mean it?"

"Sure. Try it out. It's different from the Toro because there's no engine. You just push it. But it's safer." I test his biceps and tell him, "Also, it's good for your muscles. You know, good exercise."

"You think I can do it?"

"I do. You've been cutting the grass with the power mower for two years. You're ready. The only difference is that using this one requires skill and precision."

I smile at him, half joking, half not. The only other thing you need to be is strong enough to push it. I'm pretty sure he is and there's only one way to find out.

Kyle pretends to crack his knuckles in preparation for getting ready. I dutifully laugh, and he grins at me before saying, "Okay. Off I go."

I watch as he pushes the mower over to the edge of the lawn. It takes a minute or two but soon he gets into his rhythm and then he's off to the races. I watch, slightly envious I can't join him, but that's the way it goes. He's doing a good job and having fun too. It's nice to see. Like I said, he's a good kid.

While he's cutting the grass, I reach over and pull my wheel chair close. It takes me a minute to get in and situated. When I do, I pick up my tools, wheel them into the garage and put everything away.

While I'm at it Joyce comes out and greets me with, "I see you've got a helper." She points out to the yard where Kyle has finished with the back.

He sees us and waves. "Hi, Mom." Joyce waves back. "Dad, should I do the front?"

I call back, "Yeah, that'd be good."

He starts cutting the side strip of grass on the way to the front yard. The blades quietly go swish, swish, swish as he moves forward. It's a peaceful sound, not like the loud two-cycle Toro engine roaring away.

We have a small bungalow home with a small lawn. It doesn't take long before he's finished with the side and has moved to the front of the house.

We both watch for a few moments. Then Joyce turns to

145

me and says, "Beverly from the clinic called. She says we should bring him in sometime before school starts. They want to do some more tests: check his blood, his muscle strength and how fatigued he gets. That kind of thing."

"He's doing great, today," I tell her, slightly defensive. "Look how well he's doing cutting the grass." I don't want to spoil the moment with the reality of our life, but my feeble attempt doesn't work.

Joyce is on to me in a flash and gives me a stern look. "We agreed we'd stay on top of this, remember? It's best for Kyle. You know that."

I understand what she means even though sometimes it's hard, like today, when he seems so normal. "Yeah, I know," I sigh with more than a little resignation, immediately giving in. "You're right."

The doctors are monitoring Kyle for the beginning stages of MS, like I've got. We haven't told him that he might one day get my disease. The doctors say that it could be years before it manifests itself. If ever. We just have to be ready for the day when he, like his dad, might be confined to a wheelchair. Hopefully it will be nothing more serious.

I look at the lawn and marvel at the fresh scent of mown grass. Those old lawn mowers really did superb work. "Sweetheart, you want to come up to the front yard with me?" I'm trying to mend the fences with her. It doesn't do anyone any good for us to argue about our son's situation. He needs both of us to be on the same page. "It's a pretty day out. We can go up front and watch Kyle for a while."

Joyce smiles at me and rubs my shoulder, our silent agreement that the fences are mended. "I'd like nothing better," she says, then bends and kisses me softly on the lips. I kiss her back, delighting in this stolen moment and being so close to her.

After a minute she pulls back, points and says, "Let's go check on our son."

The driveway gravel is pretty packed so it's not too hard for me and my wheelchair to roll to the front yard. We stop in the shade of a big maple tree and watch as Kyle walks back and forth, back and forth, cutting the grass as if he didn't have a care in the world. It's a pleasant moment for us. Everyone has an opinion about whether or not we should tell him that he might get multiple sclerosis. Joyce and I aren't stupid. We understand that we'll have to talk to him about it someday and eventually we will. But not today. Maybe not even tomorrow. For now my wife and I want to hold on to the present and keep things the way they are, for as long as we can. Why not? He's having a wonderful summer. You're only young once. He's ten years old. The future will be here soon enough.

Brotherly Love

We were walking home at sunset from the neighbourhood rink, skates swinging from the blades of our hockey sticks. Little Eddie was eight years old, younger than me by three years and smaller by a head and a half. He was revved up after the game since it was the first time he'd gotten to play with 'The Big Kids,' as he called us, so he was excited and talking a mile a minute while I ignored him, thinking about Christmas coming up in two days and wondering if our parents would call.

The temperature was near zero and the sun was setting into a steel grey layer of clouds on the horizon to the west, turning the sky dull pink. We were getting cold so I did something I never should have done. I had us take a short cut across the big pond that formed one edge of the boundary to the trailer park where our grandparents' double wide trailer was parked. The ice had recently formed, but I figured it'd save us ten minutes, so why not take a chance, being as cold as we were.

Cold, but thirsty. We were eating handfuls of snow as we shuffled along and I was watching a dozen or so crows flocking to roost in a dead tree on the shoreline a hundred yards away. Suddenly the ice made a sickening, groaning sound. My immediate thought was a panicky, *It's going to crack. It can't do that. Not with us out in the middle. No way.* Then my mind went to Little Eddie. If he broke through he'd be toast. He wasn't the strongest swimmer in the world.

I put my hand out and commanded, "Stop!" For once my brother obeyed me. I was about to say, "Don't move," when suddenly there was a booming THUMP and huge crack split open at our feet. In the next instant the ice gave way, plunging us into the pond, sticks and skates flying.

When I hit the water I lost my breath, it was so cold. I was fighting to regain my breathing when Eddie threw his arms around my neck in a strangle-hold. Gasping for air from both the frigid water and my brother's ever tightening grip, I grabbed for the edge of the hole, but the ice kept breaking away until I finally slipped off, pulled under by the combined weight of our waterlogged clothes. I managed to suck in a shallow gasp of air just before we sank down, down, Little Eddie clinging to me in terror, bubbles streaming from his mouth. I thought for sure we were done for and going to drown. Then miraculously my feet hit the mucky bottom.

The water was so muddy all I could see was opaque light from the hole above, but I figured we had a chance. I held Little Eddie tight, squatted down and then extended my legs fast like two pistons, shooting us upward. We broke through the surface, coughing and gasping. I tried to tread water, but my boots were so heavy I soon became exhausted. Worse, I started to lose my grip on Little Eddie. I tightened my hold on him and slung my other arm over the edge of the hole, but the ice broke and we started to sink again. Panicking, I kicked my legs as hard as I could to stay afloat, breaking through more ice before I finally found some solid enough to support us. I hung on for dear life completely spent, with no idea what to do next.

It was then I heard Little Eddie whimpering. He had turned his cold, wet face into my neck for warmth or comfort or both. He was even more terrified than I was. His raw fear jump started my will to save him. With a sudden surge of energy I didn't know I had, I kicked and pushed and shoved with all my remaining strength until I was able to lever my nearly frozen brother up out of the water and clear of the hole. He lay panting and coughing while I hung onto the edge, fighting a losing battle with the unrelenting cold.

After a few minutes Little Eddie began to revive until he was able to roll over and look at me, ice crystals forming on his wet clothes. "Rick, are you all right?"

"I'm freezing to death," I told him, my teeth chattering. "You need to get help."

"Won't we get into trouble?"

These days, when we talk about that night, my brother's statement always makes us laugh. Back then, though, our situation was too dire to be even remotely funny. I swore, "God damn it, Eddie, run and get help. Now. Fast."

He scrambled to his feet, and even though his clothes were beginning to freeze solid like icy boards, he ran like I'd never seen him run before.

I'll never forget waiting for him. Night had fallen completely and the temperature had dropped way below zero, becoming dangerously cold. My body had lost all feeling. My waterlogged boots and clothes threatened to drag me back under water at any moment. I passed into and out of consciousness as hypothermia took over. I wondered if I'd ever see my little brother again.

I finally passed out for good. I was slowly freezing to death when I thought I heard a voice. I couldn't even raise my head to look. *It's probably my imagination*, I thought. Then, I heard it again. What was going on? I forced my frozen eyelids open and saw right in front of me the face of Little Eddie. And it wasn't my imagination. He'd returned with a neighbour who had called the police. But my little brother hadn't waited safely off to the side like a prudent person would have done. Courageously, he had edged back onto the ice and laid himself out prone, extending his hand to me, "Here, Rick. Grab on." Through the fog of my near unconsciousness, I followed his instruction. I reached for my brother and felt him grasp my hand." I've got you," he said. "Hold on." And I did.

Behind him the neighbour was yelling at him to get away from the hole, but my brother ignored him. I couldn't move or respond, but it didn't matter. Little Eddie held my hand, whispered words of encouragement and stayed with me until help arrived. That's what counted. Him and me, brothers to the end, safe and together. It was the best Christmas present I ever received.

The Jump

I didn't expect so many people to be standing around on the cliff overlooking the Yellow Knife River but there were, maybe fifteen or so, mostly young folks in their twenties just hanging out, joking around and having a good time, everyone looking tan and fit. It was honestly not what I expected at all. Scared as I was, I found the festive atmosphere kind of distracting and that was a good thing, given my growing unease. *You know what*, I thought to myself, *this just might work out okay.*

Next to me my ten year old grandson took my hand and smiled. "Grandpa, look at all the people. This is really cool."

He pulled me along, ever closer to the edge. I followed behind trying to calm my rapidly beating heart, with little success. *Was I really going to do this? Was I really going to conquer my fear of heights and jump off a thirty foot cliff into a river?* It looked like I was. *If my wife could only see me now.*

A week earlier when I'd told Connie of my plan she'd said derisively, "So you've got a bucket list, Ed? First I've heard of it. And jumping off a cliff is the first thing on it? What, are you nuts?" She shook her head in marital disappointment. "Look, I asked you to take down the swing set in the backyard at the beginning of summer, what, three months ago? You couldn't be bothered. Now, suddenly you've got this ridiculous bucket list that you're all fired up about, and it has to happen like right now. What's next? Parachuting out of an airplane?" I quickly found something of interest down by my shoes and averted my gaze. How'd she known about that? It was third on the list, right after hiking the Appalachian Trail. "How about you put, 'Take down the swing set' on that stupid list of yours, huh? Maybe then it'll get done."

I tried to recover some modicum of dignity. "Look, I'm sorry about the swing set. I'll get on it right away."

"Yeah, right." I could see it in her eyes. My wife's opinion of men, never very high even on a good day, slipped down another rung on her ladder of disappointment. "Before or after you jump off the cliff?"

I felt some clarification was in order. "You know that I've always been afraid of heights. I just want to prove to myself that I can do it, and, you know, get past my fear. Plus...well, I'm jumping into a river," I said, for some reason thinking it would put a positive spin on things. Wrong.

"Oh, well, a river," she said and then let out derisive "humph," which rattled the crockery in the nearby kitchen cabinet. "Well, that makes it all right then." She thought for a moment, shaking her head, dismay written all over her face. We had a good marriage and had been together over forty years, but it wasn't out of the ordinary for me to do something to either try her patience, or disappoint her, or both. This obviously was one of those times. "Well, call Ronny at least. See if he'll go with you. Maybe our son can help protect you from yourself."

Whew. Off the hook.

I watched as she turned on her heel and headed for the living room, phone in hand, eager, I was sure, to call one of her girl friends to commiserate once again on the idiocy of the male species, a life-long pastime of theirs. Well, it wouldn't be the first time and probably not the last, either, but what could I say? At least I kept things interesting.

As if she could read my mind, Connie turned and gave me a pointed look. "What did you say?"

"Ah, nothing. I...I just..."

I shut up. It was disconcerting that the longer we were married, the more she seemed to be able to read my mind. I'd have to watch myself.

She jabbed a long, pointed finger in my direction. "Something about keeping things interesting? Is that what you said? Well, you'd better watch it, buddy, that's all I've got to say."

Scary. *Was she becoming clairvoyant?* I shuddered at the thought. That's all I needed.

I took a moment to collect myself and then called our oldest son and explained what was going on. "This Saturday? Sorry, Dad, can't go. I'm swamped at the dealership, but maybe Noah can. I'll put him on."

I took care of my grandson and his two younger sisters one day a week after school. He and I loved doing things together, and after he listened to my idea about jumping into the Yellow Knife River it took him all of about two seconds to say, "Yes!"

And that's what brought us that Saturday to the forests of central Minnesota, a two hour drive north of Minneapolis, on a warm and sunny August afternoon.

A tall, well built, dreadlocked guy who looked to be in his mid-twenties broke away from the group when he saw us walking toward the cliff's edge. He came up and smiled a greeting, "Hey there, guys. What's going on? Here to jump off Lollipop?"

His grin was infectious, and his bright white teeth were accented by his tan face. He was wearing cut-off jeans and flip flops. I tried not to stare at his bare chest and torso, rippling with muscles. He kind of looked like I imagined Hercules might have looked like. Next to me I swear Noah whispered, "Wow."

Lollipop? What the heck was he talking about? I coughed to clear my suddenly restricted throat and said, "Jump into the river? Yeah, I think I am."

He grinned, pointed to the cliff and said affectionately, "Lollipop is what we call this little baby here."

"Really?" I stammered. It was all I could think to say. Then I croaked out, "Why's that?" And why was my mouth suddenly so dry? But he was very friendly, and I was trying to be friendly back, you know, trying to get into the spirit of things. Next to me Noah surreptitiously handed me a bottle of water which I gratefully drank from.

"We call it that because it's such a sweet little jump." His grin widened. "Not like that bad boy up there." He pointed over his shoulder toward a long rise. Through the trees I could barely make out a high cliff about a hundred yards downstream.

"What's that one called?" I asked, trying to keep my voice steady.

"Hangman," he said and laughed, "because the drop could kill you."

Next to me Noah said, "Yikes," while I wiped a bead of sweat from my brow and tried to get my racing heart under control.

Mr. Dreadlocks took a long moment looking me over before he calmly patted me on the shoulder and said, "Let's get you started with Lollipop and save Hangman for some other day. How's that sound?"

The answer was obvious to me. "Sounds good," I said, trying to sound confident.

Next to me Noel whispered, "Way to go, Grandpa," as he took the bottle from my suddenly fidgety hand.

Mr. Dreadlocks then slapped me on the back (he really was a touchy-feely kind of guy) and turned to his friends, yelling, "Gang, we've got a jumper here!" A chorus of cheers arose from the crowd. He turned and gave me the thumbs up sign before giving me another once over, taking a bit more time appraising me.

I'm a little overweight (doughy would be putting it mildly) and nearly bald. I was wearing tan cargo shorts, a dark blue Minnesota Twins tee-shirt and a Twins baseball cap. On my feet I wore an old pair of canvas tennis shoes. In my research on cliff jumping, I'd read that they would help protect my feet from the force of the impact on the water.

"First time?" Like he even had to ask.

"Yeah," I said, and damn it if my voice didn't crack. I tried to recover. "It's on my bucket list."

"Bucket list? Really. Well, we get that a lot here," he grinned and stuck his hand out. "Welcome. My name's Cody."

We shook. "Hi. I'm Ed and this is my grandson, Noah." He shook Cody's hand, but didn't, or couldn't, say anything, enamoured as he was to the point of speechlessness by the statuesque Adonis standing before us.

"Great to meet you guys. If you want, I'll help you out."

"That'd be nice," I said, meaning it, my relief palpable.

For the next ten minutes or so he talked me through what he called The Jump. He was really nice about it, patient with me and informative. He seemed to understand the trepidation a sixty-five year old man might have about leaping into space.

As he talked people kept coming up to the area and jumping off the cliff, often without any warning or fanfare whatsoever. I saw a skinny whip of a girl walk to the edge, hold her nose and step right off. I saw a guy and a woman around of forty jump whilst holding hands. And then one of Cody's friends, Mia, ran off the edge and did a back flip on her way down. Watching all those jumpers served to make me both excited and nervous, a strange feeling to have.

Finally, Cody clasped me on the shoulder in a friendly way and said, "Okay Ed, that's about it." He looked me over once again and nodded to himself. "I'd say you're all set to go. How about it? Are you ready?"

156

I looked around. The sky was cloudless and clear blue. A hot sun was beating down. The scent emanating from the pine forest was heady and fragrant. The crowd nearby was boisterous and happy. I'd been coached by the inimitable Cody. I guess I was as ready as I'd ever be.

I took a deep breath. "Sure. Yeah. I'm ready."

"Super." Cody turned to the crowd and yelled, "Ed's going for it!"

There was a heartfelt cheer, and lots of "Atta boys" and "Way to gos."

I gave my hat to Noah and stepped to the edge. The river was wide, about two-hundred feet across, and even though there was a current the surface looked calm with barely a ripple showing. The sheer granite cliff I was on had formed eons ago with a natural ledge that sloped away from the edge toward the shore. All I had to do was step off and drop thirty feet straight down. I was told it would take less than two seconds before I hit the water.

I took a deep breath and exhaled. Cody had suggested not to not look down, so I didn't. I looked across the river to the pine trees and rocky cliffs on the other side. Behind me Noah whispered, "You can do it Grandpa." I felt him take my hand and squeeze.

I turned and looked at him and he smiled an encouraging smile. I smiled back, squeezed his hand once more, and let go. *Let's do this*, I said to myself. Then I turned and stepped into space.

For a moment I hung suspended. It felt like I was floating. Then I was air born and free falling, and it was exhilarating. The wind whipped past me, and I'm pretty sure I held my breath. I kept my hands glued to my sides, and the river came up fast. When I hit the water I heard my feet smack the surface as bubbles boiled around me. I went under and spread my arms and legs wide so I wouldn't go too deep. I was conscious of blowing air out through my nose to keep water from going in. Then I swam up about five feet to the surface, not having expected the water to be as cold as it was. But the coolness felt refreshing and added to my euphoria. I'd survived my jump and I was alive! I felt fantastic and energized. I couldn't believe it; I'd conquered my fear of heights. I felt a sense of accomplishment unlike any I'd ever felt before. I hope it doesn't sound too crazy to say this, but I will – I felt reborn.

I was also revelling in what must have been a natural high coupled with an adrenaline rush in the aftermath of my accomplishment; the sun seemed brighter, the sky bluer and the wild river I was floating in seemed...well, wilder. Suddenly there was a huge splash next to me. I looked over and saw Cody's head as he bobbed up to the surface. He was grinning like there was no tomorrow. "You did it, man. Welcome to the club." He gave me a high-five which I awkwardly returned.

I don't know why, but I was so happy I had tears in my eyes.

We swam to shore and climbed a trail back to the top where I was greeted with an enthusiastic outpouring of support and camaraderie by the crowd that had seemed to have doubled in size since I'd first arrived. Noah gave me a big bear hug. For an old guy who wasn't coordinated or in any kind of athletic shape, I have to say that I felt unexpectedly on top of the world. As far as checking something off a bucket list went, I'd have to say that my 'Jump off a cliff' had worked out pretty good.

Later, driving home, Noah couldn't quit talking about the whole experience; how cool Cody was. How amazing his girlfriend Mia was. How neat my jump into the river was. Finally he asked, "Can we go back again, Grandpa? If you want to, that is. If you do go, I'd like to go, too. I mean, if that'd be okay with you." He was excitedly running off at the mouth, and it was kind of cute, but I have say that I understood the feeling.

I wondered what Connie would say, me driving back north with Noah sometime and jumping off the cliff again. Well, I knew exactly what she'd say. She'd look at me like I was crazy and say, "Oh, really, Ed, jump again? What, are you completely insane? Once wasn't enough? You've got to do it again? What have you got to prove? Are you seriously trying to kill yourself?" Then she'd wonder if was time to take me in to a psychiatrist and have some tests done or something.

I'll probably never get her to understand that jumping wasn't about ego or some macho malarkey or anything like that. It was about facing a fear and overcoming it. The jump was a means to an end. Besides, it turned out to be an incredible experience.

I didn't have to think too long. To heck with it. I turned to my grandson and said, "You know what, I just might." I waited just a tick and said, "And if I do, you can come with."

"Yea! Great Grandpa," he grinned, "I can't wait."

I'm sure Noah had his own reasons for wanting to go back, but I did, too. The more I thought about it the more I figured, *Why not jump again? You only live once, no matter how crazy it might seem to others.* Besides, once I conquered my fear, it turned out that jumping was an unbelievable rush, one I wouldn't mind experiencing again. That being said, however, I'm positive I'm going to leave Hangman to those made of firmer stuff than me.

So, yeah, I think I'll go back, maybe even next weekend. And when I do, there's certainly a bright spot in it for my wife and her friends and their observations concerning the idiotic behaviour of men; it'll give them one more thing to talk about. And that's just fine. It's the least I can do, and I'm sure they'll appreciate it. So everyone will be happy, and that's got to be a good thing. Right?

But before we go, I'll get Noah to help me take down that swing set in our backyard. Promise.

Agate Hunting

After we waved good-bye to the last of the guests, Janet turned to me and asked, "Where's Evan?"

"I think he's downstairs. I got the feeling he wanted to be alone for a while. First the funeral and now the reception, I think it all got a little overwhelming."

"Why don't you go check on him? I'll fix us some supper."

We were feeling the weight of the loss of our only child, Jenny, who was also our ten year grandson's mother. We'd be taking care of him for the foreseeable future while his father recovered in the hospital from the deadly car accident that had changed our lives forever. This wasn't going to be easy for any of us.

We gave each other a hug followed by a quick kiss. "Okay. I'll go see how he's doing," I told her and went downstairs.

Evan was at my work bench looking at a jar of agates. He turned to me. "These are really neat Grandpa."

I walked up next to him and said, "They really are, aren't they? I polished them in my rock tumbler a long time ago, way before you were born."

I watched as he continued to study them. He seemed interested, so it gave me an idea. "Come with me, I want to show you something." We went to my office and I reached up on a shelf above my desk. Out of the corner of my eye I watched as Evan followed my every move. "Here, have a look at this," I said, handing him a clear glass jar.

"He peered closely at its contents. What is that, Grandpa?"

"Check it out. Open it."

He did and reached in to pull out a walnut sized stone and began to admire it in the palm of his hand. His eyes grew wide open. "Wow. This is really cool. What is it?"

"It's a Lake Superior agate."

He studied it carefully. "It's really pretty."

I smiled. "Yeah it is. It's a favourite of mine."

"Where'd you get it?"

"I found this when I was about your age on a gravel road in northern Minnesota. It was my first agate. Feel how smooth it is."

He rubbed the stone between his hands like he was warming it up. Then he held it close and gazed with wonder at the rusty red hues enfolding swirls of white crystals. I didn't blame him. It was a beautiful specimen.

I said, "To me, it's like holding a piece of magic. It was formed from volcanic fires and lava flows millions of years ago where Lake Superior is now located."

"But that's way up north. How'd it get to where you found it on that gravel road?"

I smiled, enjoying that he was momentarily distracted from his mother's death. "Can you imagine that it somehow made its journey to that road by the long, slow movement of the glaciers? I prefer to think of it as part glaciation, part mystery." He continued studying the agate as I carried on, "It's hard to find them these days. They're very unique, and their value is in their rarity." I loved talking about rocks, much to the consternation of my wife. It was nice to have a captive audience.

He laughed. "You're talking weird, Grandpa. Like poetry or something."

"Well, to me there's something special about them," I chuckled along with him. "Call it poetry or magic or whatever, but I'm glad that you like it as much as I do." I paused for a moment, enjoying how happy the stone was making him feel. Then I made a quick decision. "I'll tell you what, you can keep it. It's yours."

He visibly gasped and his eyes lit up. "No way! Really?"

"Yep. It's a cool agate. Enjoy it."

"Oh, Grandpa, thank you so much. It's beautiful. I love it."

He was happy for the first time since the tragic car accident that had killed his mother. Then he threw his arms around my neck and gave me a big hug. I hugged him right back. Tight.

After a minute I led him back to the work bench and we sat down on a couple of stools. I told him a little bit more about agates and their history as he gently caressed the singular stone he held in his small hands, his thoughts for a moment taken away from this sad day.

When I was finished he was quiet. I was, too. What would each of our lives be like now that someone we both loved so dearly was no longer with us? My Jenny. Evan's mother.

After a minute he looked at me hopefully and asked, "Grandpa? Do you think we could maybe go searching for more agates sometime? It would be so fun. I'd really like to do that."

His innocence and quiet voice almost broke my heart. We were both suffering and grieving our loss. Evan picked up the jar of polished agates he'd first been looking at and held it up, reverently turning it back and forth to catch the light and show the colours of the stones inside, gazing at them entranced, as if in another world.

It would be so easy to say, "Sure, let's do that. Let's go hunting agates." And I almost did, but then I was held back by a sudden, horrible thought. *What if I said "Yes" and we went up north we didn't find any? Agates were hard to find nowadays. The disappointment might crush him.*

"Maybe we should wait awhile," I suggested.

"Aw..." He set the jar down and turned away, but not before I could see tears forming in his sad eyes. "Okay," he sighed.

I mentally pinched myself. What a jerk I was being for

refusing to take my grandson on a trip we could both use just because I was afraid of a little disappointment. We'd just buried a person we both loved dearly for Pete's sake. Not find any agates? I'm sure I could deal with that. Same with Evan. I had to give us both a little credit.

"Wait a minute," I told him, putting my hand on his shoulder. "I take that back." He turned to me and his eyes became wide with anticipation. "Sure," I said, "let's do it. Let's go find ourselves some agates."

"Are you sure, Grandpa? Really?" The way his face lit up and the happiness that shone in his eyes made me realize I'd made the right decision.

"Absolutely," I said, instantly planning a driving trip north and picturing him cradling a handful of newly found agates in his cupped palms. "Let's go tomorrow."

"Yea!" he shouted and started dancing around the room.

Just then Janet called from upstairs. "You two all right down there?"

I looked at Evan and he looked back at me. We were both grinning. "Yeah," I said. "We're just fine."

"Okay, then. Supper's ready. Come on."

"Goody, I'm famished," Evan said. He ran ahead and hurried up the steps, clutching the agate I'd given him and yelling, "Grandma, look what Grandpa gave me."

I smiled at my departing grandson. "I'll be up in a minute," I called after him, but I doubt he heard me.

I went to the work bench to turn off the light and saw the jar of agates with the top open. *What the heck*, I thought to myself. I grabbed a few before putting the lid back on. It wouldn't hurt to have some on hand to scatter on the ground up north for us to find. Just in case. Evan didn't need any more disappointments in his young life. Not now. At least not if I could help it.

164

The Inn on the Lake

"Sam, don't forget to lock the door."

"I won't." He slung his backpack over his shoulder, clicked the key fob for the Ford Focus and added, muttering under his breath, "I'm not an idiot, you know."

Mary might have been old, but she could still hear well enough to give him a sharp look.

Oh, oh, he thought to himself, *now she's probably ticked off at me.* But Mary didn't say anything in response. He watched as she turned and marched determinedly through the rain and parking lot puddles to the front entrance of where the two them would be staying, the Inn on the Lake. *Then again, maybe not. It might just be my imagination.*

He opened his umbrella and followed, wondering in the back of his mind how this planned outing of theirs was going to go. He hoped well, but you never knew, especially after fifty-three years of marriage. Well, hold on; after all those years he knew exactly how it was going to go. Even if she was mad at him her bad mood would soon pass. They were too old to let little things like that bother them for long. It would go just fine.

Mary flipped her long grey braid over the outside of her yellow rain jacket and met him just inside the entrance, holding the door open. "Did you bring my umbrella with you? I'm going to need it if we're going for a walk along the shore after we check in."

"Why didn't you bring it yourself? You knew it was raining," he chided her, giving her a hard time, hoping to dissipate the little scene in the parking lot. He shook out his umbrella, closed it and set it aside.

"Well, Sam, I can't be expected to remember everything, can I?" She bit off her words, her eyes fiery. She wasn't willing to give in.

"Well, you certainly expect me to."

She sighed resignedly and shook her head. She was about ready to argue some more when she suddenly laughed. Sam had reached into his pack and pulled her umbrella out from where he'd hidden it. He opened it and handed it over to her, flourishing it like a magician with a bunch of flowers. "Here you go my little chickadee," he said in the poorest imitation of W.C. Fields anyone had ever heard. "An umbrella bouquet just for you."

"Oh, shush, you," she said, grabbing the umbrella and trying unsuccessfully to sound mad. "And act your age, you old coot." Her grin, though, gave her away, the earlier scene in the parking lot now completely forgotten.

They stepped off to the side to let a young couple with two small children squeeze past. Mary closed her umbrella as she watched the little family. She pointed to the kids and said, "Remember when James, Annie and Tim were that young? Those were good times."

He was happy to see her bad mood had vanished. They were both seventy-eight years old. Their three kids were in their late forties and early fifties and in total they had six grandchildren aged sixteen to twenty-six. The time she was referring to was so far in the past that he'd completely forgotten about it.

But if he told her he didn't remember, he was positive she'd be all over him. "Sure," he said, "those were great times."

Mary smiled, squeezed his arm and led him inside for check in. "No you don't, Mr. Sam Baker. You can't fool me, but that's okay. I won't hold it against you."

They crossed a lobby that was more than welcoming. On the left was a comfortable seating area filled with overstuffed chairs and conveniently placed end tables. The focal point was a wall mounted gas fireplace lit with flames cheerfully flickering. Without speaking they looked at each other and silently agreed. The Inn was going to be perfect for what they had in mind.

They approached the counter where a young man in a dark maroon sports coat was waiting. Mary whispered to Sam, "You did remember to bring the Declaration, didn't you?"

"Yes, I did." He pointed to his backpack. "It's right there. All set for us to review."

"Hush, now," Mary said, schussing him. "We'll talk about it later."

He whispered back, "Okay." Then he turned to the young man at the counter, pulled his worn leather wallet out of his back pocket, took out a credit card and laid it on the counter.

The young man whose name tag read 'Gary' glanced at it, smiled and said, "Welcome to the Inn on the Lake. How may I help you today?" He was college aged, nice and polite. Sam could see Mary was impressed by his friendly attitude. Sam was too for that matter.

"Reservation for the Bakers. One night only with a lake view room," Sam stated. Gary busied himself getting the paperwork ready. Sam glanced at Mary and leaned towards her, saying under his breath, "Not only the Declaration, but I remembered my wallet, too. I'm not an idiot, you know."

Mary grinned. "Not all the time, but I love you anyway." Then she changed the subject and whispered in his ear, "We'll talk about the Declaration later today, all right?"

"Sounds good," he whispered back.

He was about to say more when Rick Jorgenson stepped from his office behind the counter and hurried towards them, extending his hand in a warm greeting. "Sam and Mary, welcome. I thought I heard your voices." He was tall and robust, with a neatly trimmed beard, short cropped hair and the ruddy complexion of an outdoorsman. "How are my two favourite lodgers?"

Sam and Mary dutifully laughed at his joke. The Inn on the Lake is three stories high, over two hundred feet long and has one hundred and seventy nine guest rooms. The two of them had been coming to it for over thirty years and have known Rick for the last five, ever since he'd been manager. Sam's guess is he had more than a few favourite guests.

They played along just for fun. "We're just great, Rick," Sam said at the exact moment Mary responded with, "We're wonderful. Happy to be here."

They all laughed like one big happy family and then made small talk. Rick spoke about the weather, saying "It's been better," and that the business was "Super good."

When the check-in paperwork was completed, Gary interrupted their conversation, with, "Okay. You're all set."

He handed them their key cards and Sam and Mary said goodbye. They crossed the lobby and took the elevator to the third floor where they walked down the hallway to the same room they'd been coming to every time they stayed at the Inn. They dropped their bags off and Sam grabbed his daypack. Ten minutes later they were back downstairs and outside.

Mary was still in her yellow rain jacket and he'd changed into a dark blue one. He'd also put on his Minnesota Twins baseball hat. They were ready for whatever the weather had to offer and right now it was misting. Heavily. So with their umbrellas lifted and pointed into a slight breeze, they began to walk along the shore of beautiful Lake Superior, the largest of the great lakes and the biggest freshwater lake in the world.

They were walking on a wooden boardwalk that followed the shoreline for over half a mile from where they

168

were at Canal Park to downtown Duluth, and then five miles further up the far shoreline almost to the Glensheen Mansion. The Inn was near one end of the boardwalks, only a quarter of a mile from two white lighthouses, the shipping canal and famed Duluth Harbor lift bridge that ushered ore freighters and pleasure craft into and out of the Port of Duluth.

"Oh, I so love it here," Mary said enthusiastically, stopping after only a minute or so of walking. She turned to look out over the vast lake while wiping some moisture from her forehead. She was just over five feet tall and had pretty eyes, a wide mouth and high cheekbones, a distinctive look handed down over generations by her Sami ancestors from northern Finland. She was wearing jeans, hiking boots and a light blue cotton sweater under her jacket. Three foot high swells were rolling in, crashing on the rocky shore only thirty feet from them. Their booming thunder filled the air, almost, but not quite, drowning out the calls of the white gulls circling above them. "Sam, everything is just like I wanted it to be. It's perfect. Just perfect." She turned to him and smiled, wiping more mist from her face. "I think this is my favourite place in the whole wide world." She gazed out over the lake again for a few moments before she turned to him and asked, "How long have we been coming here, again?"

He'd kept a daily journal ever since they'd been married and had consulted it before their trip, hoping for a chance to show that his memory wasn't really as bad as everyone thought it was, although, if he were perfectly honest, it was. "We've been coming here at least once a year for thirty one years," he announced proudly. "This is our thirty second year."

"My, oh, my. Over thirty years," Mary said contemplatively, as she turned back to the view. "And all those times I was with you and not with my secret boyfriend. Imagine that," she glanced sideways at him, wearing what he can only describe as an impish grin.

"Lucky me," he smiled back at her.

He liked it when she joked like she was doing right now. It offset the times when her depression was so severe she could hardly move from whatever spot she'd chosen to sit or lie in, let alone talk to him and make jokes.

Suddenly she grabbed his arm and pulled him close. He could feel the fabric of her jacket against his own, even catch a whiff of the scent she wore, something light with a hint of sandalwood. It was times like now, when her depression was at bay and his mind was working clearly, that he appreciated the most, especially at this stage of their lives.

She gave him a quick peck on the cheek, smiled, and then turned back to the lake to enjoy the view.

In college, Mary trained to become a registered nurse and was hired right out of school to work at Hennepin County Medical Center, a huge complex in downtown Minneapolis. She was assigned to various areas in the sprawling facility during her thirty-seven years of employment, but ended up spending most of her time on the sixth floor Burn Ward administering to victims sixty-five percent of whom never recovered. She was a compassionate nurse, calmly taking care of her patients, helping to ease not only their physical pain, but their emotional trauma as well.

Sam fell in love with her when they first met at the University of Minnesota. He was finishing up his degree in biology and had decided to get a teaching certificate in case he didn't get a job working at his preferred professional choice as a wildlife biologist for the Minnesota Department of Natural Resources. Mary had, at one time, also contemplated teaching and they met in a class they were both enrolled in,

170

Introduction to Learning Methodology. After three years of dating they married in nineteen sixty four and bought a home in southwest Minneapolis a few years later.

Sam never got that job with the DNR. Instead, he became a teacher and taught biology at Southwest High School in Minneapolis for thirty six years, retiring in the year two thousand. Mary followed suit a few years later and they have lived happily ever since, gardening, bird watching and walking the streets of their quiet Minneapolis neighbourhood. They couldn't have been happier.

They were also getting older and slowing down. Sam's memory was not what it used to be and his heart was functioning at seventy percent of its capacity due to congestive heart failure. He also had his right hip replaced a few years ago so he walked with a slight limp. He hadn't yet given in to using a cane.

Mary's physical heath was still good but her mental health was failing. Thankfully, her good days still outnumbered her bad ones.

When it came to their advancing age they were finding ways to cope. One of those ways was to make their annual journey to the Inn on the Lake to enjoy the majesty of Lake Superior, a lake they have come to love and where they'd built a treasure trove of memories.

"Sam, look over there," Mary said, suddenly, pointing.

He looked. About three hundred yards from shore were three brightly-coloured kayaks. They were fighting through the swells, working their way from left to the right. "Must be heading for the canal," Sam said. "Maybe they're going into the harbour." He watched them skilfully manoeuvre the waves, feeling slightly envious. It looked like it was fun, if not more than a little dangerous.

Mary turned and set off walking. "Let's hurry and watch them go through the canal."

Her idea sounded like fun and Sam silently cursed his gimpy hip as he turned to follow. "Slow down," he called out when she quickly outpaced him. "I'm hobbling as fast as I can."

She turned and waved. "I'll meet you," she grinned and continued.

"Go for it, Speedy," he muttered, and resigned himself to never catching up to his fast walking wife.

He wasn't mad, though, because it was good to be outside with her. They were next to the lake they loved, and they were breathing fresh northern Minnesota air. Plus, he was as mobile as he could be. He gritted his teeth and hobbled on, glad to have some time to think about the real reason they were at the lake they loved so much.

Oregon's Death with Dignity Act was enacted in nineteen ninety-seven. When it came into law Sam and Mary were in their late fifties and weren't thinking much about end of life questions, other than completing their wills and making sure each of them was taken care of should one precede the other in death. And, of course, they also made sure their kids were taken care of. Like most people, however, once their wills were completed, they only revisited them every year or two like a lawyer friend suggested. Mainly, they just got on with their lives.

All was fine until their twenty-two-year-old grandson Will was killed in two thousand and two by hostile fire in eastern Afghanistan. Willie's dad and mom, their son, James and his wife Abby, were, of course, devastated. They helped them cope with their grief as much as they could, but some wounds never healed.

San knew for certain Mary's depression was tied to Willie's death. In fact, she'd told him as much many times, only recently saying, "I just can't shake how sad I am that Willie is gone. He was such a fine young man and had his whole life ahead of him." At the time of that conversation it had been fifteen years since Will's death.

Willie really was a good boy and certainly much too young to die, but his death triggered a further deepening of the depression Mary had been saddled with her entire life, stretching as far back as her high school days. She fought her tendency towards what she called 'The Blues' every day of her life with only minimum use of medication. Due to Mary's years as a nurse and Sam's interest in science, they were both extremely attuned to the negative consequences of addiction. On the rare occasions she did have to medicate she said, "I'm only using these stupid pills to get over those bumps in the road I can't cope with. You know that, right? You really don't have to worry about me, I'm fine."

Sam understood her. It wasn't the pills he was worried about, it was her depression. They were coping, but that still didn't mean that he didn't worry about her.

Sam had his right hip replaced about ten years after Willie's death. These days he walked slowly, but was happy to at least be able to move as well as he could. His big issue now was with his memory. "Or lack of it," as he would say. "If only I wasn't quite so forgetful."

Some would suggest he had early onset Alzheimer's and he'd probably agree. He'd been tested and but the conclusions were vague and nothing could be proven as definitive. All the doctors he'd talked with agreed when they told him that he was getting older and memory loss was associated with aging. He believed them because he was living proof that it happened.

Four years ago Mary and Sam watched a special on their local Public Broadcasting channel about Oregon's Death with Dignity legislation. It got them thinking: *What would we do if we had a choice about not only when to die, but how to die?* Over the next few months they talked about it almost non-stop and came up to this conclusion: since they did have a choice they might as well do something about it.

So they did.

They made up another will; a document, really, and called it Our Right to Die Declaration. In it they stipulated that they were mentally competent to make their own decision regarding ending each of their lives and they were going to do so when the time came. They signed it and dated it, but getting their Declaration notarized was not possible. They tried it once and got some very strange looks. They were also on the receiving end of one rather uncomfortable visit from a concerned police officer that an overly vigilant notary public had called. A person who, in Sam and Mary's opinion, seemed to take their job a little too seriously as far as they were concerned.

The statement in the document, 'When the time comes', was what brought Mary and Sam to Duluth and Lake Superior on this particular visit. They planned to discuss if now was the right time. They'd even brought along sleeping tablets in case they decided that the answer was yes.

Mary stopped half way to the canal, turned and hurried back to Sam, who was moving slower than usual. He was also panting and his heart was starting to labour, not a good thing given his congestive heart failure issues.

"I'm so sorry, Sam. I didn't mean to run off like that," she said, coming up to him and looking concerned. "I was just so excited. I'll slow down and walk with you." She took his arm and tugged on it.

"No, don't worry about it," he said, trying to hide his shortness of breath and hoping to appear like a normal, healthy old person, whatever that was.

Mary didn't buy it. "Really, Boss Man," a term of endearment she used that he especially liked, but couldn't tell you why. "It's okay. Seriously. I'll try to walk more slowly and keep you company."

Sam looked around, suddenly conscious of people moving past them and wondered: *Are these people listening to our discussion? Are they watching us? If they are, they probably think we're probably a couple of addled escapees from some Senior Center down the road trying to figure out which way is up.*

Mary started to pull him along beside her, but he stopped her. "Really. Just go on ahead. It's fine. I'm fine. Seriously. I'm just taking my time."

She looked at him judging his sincerity and saw he wasn't kidding. She knew he liked it when she was enthusiastic about something like the kayakers. After a moment she sensed that her husband was all right with her going ahead on her own.

She released his arm. "Ok, Boss Man. If you're sure."

He motioned for her to continue without him. "I am. Promise. I'll be right behind."

"Ok, then. Just take it easy."

"I will."

Before she left she handed him her umbrella. The mist had almost stopped, so he folded it up and put it in his day pack. Then he did the same with his own. He could tell Mary was excited to get closer to the kayakers so he reaffirmed that he'd be all right. "Really," he encouraged her. "Just go ahead."

She grinned and gave his arm a squeeze, then thought twice and gave him a quick hug. "Take it easy with that heart of yours," she cautioned and then hurried off. He followed, moving slowly and steadily, lagging behind, but conscious of taking it easy like Mary told him to do.

It took about ten minutes to join Mary near the Maritime Visitors Center located next to canal and the lift bridge where she met him, after waving good-bye to the kayakers.

"Having a good time?" he asked as she hurried over.

"The best ever," Mary grinned enthusiastically. "I'm having a wonderful time."

"Me, too," Sam said. He was serious. He loved it when Mary was happy.

They walked over to the breakwater and looked out across the lake. The clouds had dissipated and the sky was clear. It was the last week of September and the green leaves on the trees along the far shoreline over a mile away were starting to change to colours of orange and red and yellow and gold. The two of them silently took in the quiet splendour of the beginning of the fall season in northern Minnesota; colours so pretty they took their breaths away.

After a few minutes the mood was broken when Sam's stomach started to growl. He attempted to divert Mary's attention by pointing out a particularly interesting pebble next to his walking shoe, but nothing got past his observant wife. She asked, innocently, "What time is it?"

He checked his pocket watch, a special gift from his oldest son three years ago on his seventy fifth birthday. "It's a little after one."

"I'm getting hungry," Mary said. "Let's go get something to eat."

"Sounds fantastic. How about Amazing Grace?" he suggested.

Mary nodded in agreement. "Do you even have to ask?"

He laughed because, no, he really didn't.

Amazing Grace was a quaint little cafe that reminded them of the coffee houses they used to frequent in college back in the sixties. It took about ten minutes to walk there. They went down a short set of steps and stepped back in time. The cosy cafe had low ceilings, mismatched but comfortable chairs and wooden floors. There was even a lingering scent of incense in the air, mixing with the aroma of freshly baked goods and homemade soup. Each table had its own unique oil table cloth.

It was the kind of place where you seated yourself, so they chose a table that had a traditional red and white chequered pattern. There were a couple of fresh sprigs of purple asters in a little jam jar in the middle. They sat next to a window so they could look outside at the feet of people walking by if they wanted to, which they didn't. Sam took off his hat and hung it on the back of his chair while they made themselves comfortable waiting for someone to come to take their order.

Sam was enjoying listening to *Like a Rolling Stone* playing quietly through the overhead sound system, when Mary asked, "Did you bring the Declaration?"

He patted his daypack on the floor next and said, "Yep. Got it right here."

"Let's take a look at it after we've ordered," Mary said, then put her finger to her lips as the young man who apparently was their waitperson quickly approached and set down a glass of water for each of them.

"Hi," he said, smiling. "My name's Sean."

He was ready to hand them a couple of menus when Mary looked up and gave him a smile in return. "Hi, there, Sean. No need for a menu. I think we already know what we want."

"Ah, you've been here before," he grinned. "Great. What can I get for you?"

After their order was given, Sam reached into his daypack for the Declaration. Mary put her hand on his arm, stopping him.

"Oh, honey, I've changed my mind. Let's not bother with that right now," she said, looking at him with pleading eyes. "Is that Okay?" She rubbed his arm and smiled affectionately. "I'm having too good a time. Maybe we can wait until we get back to the room." She looked at him, her amber eyes full of light, still as beautiful to him as they were all those years ago when they first met. "Is that all right with you?"

Anything to make her happy, was Sam's immediate thought. "Sure," he reassured her. "Absolutely." He squeezed her hand and they paused like that for a few moments, looking fondly into each other's eyes, just like they used to do back in their early years together. Their shared affection right then over fifty years later felt good. Special.

After a few moments Mary squeezed Sam's hand, released it and sat back in her chair, smiling. "Let's just enjoy the rest of the day. Okay?"

He grinned back her. "I'm all for it."

With discussion of whether or not tonight they would agree to end their lives, temporarily put on hold, they leisurely enjoyed a tasty lunch. Mary was appreciative of how attentive yet unobtrusive young Sean was, so when they were finished Sam left him a healthy tip.

They were on their way out of the door when they were enticed by the cafe's bakery display. They couldn't help it; both of them were suckers for sweets. Sam purchased four cookies, chocolate chip, oatmeal raisin, lavender sugar and ginger spice and put the bag in his day pack and said good-bye to Sean.

"You have a good day," he told them in return.

"We will," Sam said, happy to have the Declaration discussion put on hold for a while.

"We're going to take the boardwalk all the way to Fitger's," Mary told him.

"Cool," he said. "Check out the bookstore up there. It's pretty good."

"We will," Sam said, appreciating his advice and not

bothering to tell him that they tried to go to Northern Lights Books every time they came to Duluth.

They waved a final goodbye and stepped into a gloriously beautiful day. The sky had completely cleared, and the temperature was a balmy sixty degrees. Sam pulled the brim of his hat down to shield his eyes from the bright sunshine. It was warm enough for them to stop and take off their jackets. Sam's flannel shirt and tee-shirt would be more than adequate for him; Mary's sweater was fine for her. Both their jackets barely fit into Sam's now nearly full day pack, and he was pondering whether to stop at their room to empty it when Mary interrupted his thoughts.

"Sean was such a nice boy," Mary said wistfully as they walked to the corner and waited for the light to change. "He reminded me of Willie a little bit."

Oh, oh.

Sam glanced at her with trepidation, wondering if her statement might signify the dip in her mood, the beginning of a downward slide towards the blues if not further into deeper depression. But, fortunately, it looked like he'd jumped the gun a little prematurely. Mary was smiling as she was talking and still happy.

In fact, she looked at Sam as if reading his mind and said, "What? I can't make a comment about a young man near to our grandson's age?" She looked at Sam and grinned. "Don't worry, Boss Man, I'm doing just fine, thank you."

Then she turned away with a big smile on her face, taking in the scene of quaint shops and tasty restaurants, all within view of Lake Superior. She took a deep breath and sighed a happy sigh, exclaiming, "Everything is so perfect. I'm so happy to be here. I love the lake, especially when the waves are breaking like they are on the rocks. Lunch was wonderful and Sean was a really good guy, too." She

179

looked at Sam with what he would swear was the same impish gleam in her eye from earlier and added, "It's good to be alive."

A fleeting image of their Right to Die Declaration appeared in Sam's mind at that moment and then, just as quickly, disappeared, as if carried by an offshore breeze out over Lake Superior. He decided not to pursue it.

The light changed. They crossed the street and walked down the sidewalk on the far side of Canal Street, the road closest to the lake and the one their hotel was on. In a minute or so they were at the Inn's parking lot.

"Should I run our jackets up to the room?" Sam asked, kind of dreading it since for some reason he was getting winded pretty easily today.

Mary didn't bat an eye. "Why don't you let me do it? You save that hip of yours for our walk. Your heart, too."

They were planning to go for a walk on the boardwalk and enjoy the sunshine and the rest of the day. Mary's idea was a good one and Sam gratefully agreed. He took their jackets out of his pack and handed them to her. She hurried towards the front door, calling over her shoulder, "I'll meet you around the back. Find a bench by the lake and sit down and take it easy. I'll just be a minute."

Thankful to get a chance to rest Sam yelled, "Ok," and slowly glimpsed around the side of the Inn to the boardwalk. He found a bench with a nice view of the lake and gratefully sat down to enjoy the scenery, the sunshine, the waves breaking along the shoreline with the gulls soaring overhead. It was not a stretch for him to imagine he and Mary easily spending many days right where they were, meandering around, enjoying the out of doors and each other's company.

He'd only booked the room for one night and was now pondering the possibility of perhaps adding another day to their stay. Suddenly, the thought occurred to him: *Wait a minute; we've still got to talk about the Declaration and what we're going to do.*

Mary tapped him on the shoulder from behind, startling him. "What do you think, Boss Man? Shall we go for a walk? Maybe got up to Fitger's? Check out the bookstore and get some ice cream?"

"Absolutely," he said, and immediately decided to hold off on his idea of staying an extra day. They still had a lot to talk about.

Mary helped him to his feet and they began walking along the boardwalk. They took their time. Sam bought a bag of popcorn and gave it to Mary to feed the seagulls. They picked through stones on the shore, looking for agates. They enjoyed watching young people diving off an old dock into the cold water. It took them about an hour to walk about a mile and they enjoyed every minute of it.

The wooden boardwalk ended and was replaced by a ten foot wide tarred path. The area became hilly and the path twisted and turned, dipped and rose, all the while maintaining a height of around twenty feet above the shore of the lake. The views were stunning with Superior on their right and the buildings of downtown Duluth only a quarter of a mile away to the left, hidden from view by beautifully landscaped gardens and trees.

Every few steps seemed to bring a new exclamation of wonder to their lips. Nearby were granite rock outcroppings accenting clumps of green pines and golden leaved aspen trees. There were colourful flower gardens packed with purple and white asters and yellow black eyed Susans. Every now and then a swathe of green lawn provided a comfortable spot for people to rest and have a picnic, of which more than a few people were doing.

Waves rolled in from across the lake in three or four

foot swells and crashed against the rocky shoreline, booming with abandon, at times tossing spray nearly as high as the path. Gulls soared above, gliding gently on the wind, wings barely moving. The sky was deep blue, the sun was shining brightly and water was glistening like an infinite sea of sparkling diamonds. It was a day worth treasuring.

At the top of a rise they came upon a wooden bench. They sat down and looked out over the vastness of the lake, enjoying an unobstructed view. For Sam and his sore hip, it felt good to rest. After about fifteen minutes Mary said, "How are you doing Boss Man? Do you want to forget about going to Fitger's and head back to the Inn instead?"

Even though he'd had a few twinges of pain in his hip and was slightly winded, he was having too good a time to call it a day. "No, I'm doing good. I love being here."

Mary laughed. She understood he wasn't exactly being honest, but she cut him some slack; she knew how much he was enjoying being on what everyone in the state of Minnesota called 'The North Shore'. "Ok, Boss Man," she said. "Let's rest a little longer, and then we'll keep going."

She patted him on the thigh and turned to look over the lake stretched out in front of them. There were a couple of charter fishing launches heading from left to right towards Duluth Harbor. In spite of their size, they looked like the toy boats kids might play with in a bath tub, so dwarfed were they by Superior's immensity, stretching to the far shoreline of Wisconsin twenty miles away. Beyond that the lake disappeared into the distant horizon. Somewhere beyond their view was Ontario, Canada. The swells rolled in and continued to crash against the rocky shoreline beneath them. Gulls circled above, calling and squawking. Where they were right now was, as Mary had said time and time that day, the perfect place for them to be and the two of them watched in companionable silence, perfectly at ease.

After a while Mary glanced at her watch and commented, "It's nearly three. Do you think you can make it the rest of the way?"

Sam was rejuvenated and ready to go. "Try and stop me," he said, getting to his feet, joints cracking. He steadfastly pointed himself down the path. "Lead on."

"I'll race you," she joked. "How's that sound? I'll even give you a head start."

"You're on." Sam grinned and hobbled off, trying to hide the grimace on his face. His hip hurt, but not so badly that he was going to let it ruin their afternoon. One thought popped into his mind, though. *If they sell canes at Fitger's, today might just be the day I decide to get one.*

Mary was kidding about racing. She grabbed hold of his shoulder to stop him from hurting himself. She'd always been conscious of his health and did what she could to make sure he ate right and didn't push himself too hard. On this glorious afternoon she made sure they took a leisurely stroll, not wanting to take any chances on injuring Sam's hip.

About every minute or so they saw individuals walking or jogging or bike riding, as well as couples out enjoying the late afternoon, just like they were. Mary took hold of Sam's arm as they walked, utterly at peace.

She looked at him and grinned. "I'm so happy."

"Me, too. I wouldn't change a thing."

She gave him a kiss on the cheek. "Best day in a long time."

"I agree." He squeezed her arm affectionately, thinking for the hundredth time today, just how lucky he was.

It took them fifteen minutes to go a quarter of a mile, but they didn't mind at all. Their buoyant mood carried them all the way to a stairway leading from the path up to

Fitger's, a former brewery now converted to shops and restaurants. Sam paused and looked at the iron steps and balked. The circular two story structure was exceptionally strong and sturdy; he and Mary had walked up it many times. Today, however, he was afraid the climb was going to be too much. Although he wanted to, he just didn't have the strength or the energy to make it to the top.

"I think I'll just rest," he said to Mary and made his way to a nearby bench where he gratefully plopped down, letting loose with a contented sigh. He took a bottle of water from his day pack, uncapped it, and took a refreshing drink. "You go on up. See if you can find us a good book or two at Northern Lights." He handed the bottle to Mary who took a drink before handing it back to him.

She made a quick decision. "Ok, Boss Man. I'll go ahead without you, but I won't be long. Just don't go flirting with any young girls while I'm gone." She laughed and leaned over and gave him quick kiss on the cheek.

He chuckled at the implausibility of her statement. "Not on your life. You're the only young lady in my life. You know that."

Mary grinned. "I know, and you'd better believe it, mister." She squeezed his shoulder affectionately before walking over to the stairway and beginning her climb. "See you in a few minutes."

Sam watched her prance up the stairs like a petite gazelle, marvelling at her energy. When she reached the top, nearly twenty feet above him, she leaned over the railing and waved. He waved back. Then she disappeared from view, making her way along the path at the top of the ridge to the back entrance to Fitger's. He sighed. *If only to be young and spry again. Or at least to be able prance like my wife.*

Then he admonished himself. Wait a minute. Who was

he to complain? It had been a good day and he was in a great mood. He was enjoying goofing around and joking with Mary. Things could have been a lot worse.

He'd learned over the years that good days like today were something to appreciate and cherish. It wasn't always like that, especially when her depression was severe. But when she was having a good time, like right now, he intended to make the most of it, for both of their sakes.

Sam's bench was on an overlook, high above the Lake, at least thirty feet above the water. Not more than fifteen feet in front of him a steep cliff led down to the rocky shore below, precluding anyone but the most adventurous, or foolhardy, from making the climb down to the water. Just as Sam was wondering if anyone was ever reckless enough to attempt such an undertaking, wouldn't you know it, two boys and a girl around twelve years old came flying along the path on skateboards, jumped off them and disappeared over the edge, skateboards securely positioned under their arms. He could hear them laughing all the way, as they climbed down to the lake.

He panicked a little, the parent in him mouthing a silent prayer that they didn't get injured. Then he realized that he was just being foolish. The kids were happy and carefree and on this beautiful fall afternoon didn't appear to have a care in the world. Who could blame them? He decided to try to forget about at least ten possible catastrophes that immediately came to his mind. Who was he to be an old fuddy-duddy to rain on their youthful parade?

Sam was pondering the advantages of being youthful and energetic when he had another and decidedly more troubling thought. For some reason, their Right to Die Declaration popped into his mind, scouring it clean of all notions of youthful enthusiasm and indiscretion. The reality of the here and now reared its ugly head. The real question facing Mary and him at this particular moment on this particular day on this particular shoreline of beautiful Lake Superior was this: Was tonight going to be the night they took out their stash of sleeping pills, drunk them down with a glass of water, fell into each other's arms and held each other close as they said goodbye to their life together? Was this the night they were going to end it all?

Sam's thoughts went something like this: Mary was in such a good mood right today and her spirits were bright and she wasn't even close to being depressed. So his guess was that she would vote to stay alive for another year. And why not? All was going well for her, or at least as well as could be expected. Nothing to worry about, right?

Then he remembered that just one month ago she had been a totally different person, having been struck almost catatonic by a fall into deep depression. Her despair was so pervasive that her mind literally went numb. She didn't interact. She didn't talk. She just lay in bed with the curtains drawn and slept. All Sam could do was try to get her to eat some soup and drink some water, nurse her along as best he could and pray she would recover like she always had in the past. Anything he did for her she struggled against. All she wanted to do was pull the blankets up over her head and close out the world. It was troubling as well as horribly frightening.

And it wasn't the first time she'd been like that either; in such a state where she seemed to have given up the will to live. Over the past few years those episodes had been happening more and more frequently. Six months ago when Mary brought them up to her psychiatrist, the doctor only prescribed different anti-depressant medication along with the admonition to, "Don't let yourself get too down." Easy for the doctor to say. Unfortunately, the new meds did nothing for poor Mary.

In fact, in the last six months, whenever she got

186

depressed, nothing seemed to help, not medications or doing things she usually enjoyed doing, like reading or gardening, or sewing or quilting; not seeing their kids or grandchildren. Nothing.

But then, snap your fingers, and, just like that, she'd pop right out of it. She'd get up, get out of bed and start living life as if nothing had happened, even though she knew something had.

That's what occurred last month. She suddenly sat up, stretched, and got out of bed, all smiling and energetic. She greeted Sam and the new day with, "Hey there, Boss Man, I'm hungry. Let's go out to eat."

Sam was overjoyed. They went to a favourite restaurant where Mary wolfed down a double serving of eggs Benedict and drank cup after cup of English Breakfast tea. Life started up for them again.

Since that last relapse Mary had been doing fine, but who knew when another episode would occur? The answer to the question was obvious; no one knew. It could happen anytime, but even if no one knew when it would happen, Mary and Sam both knew the awful truth – it would happen. And the real question was, given all that they knew, did Mary want to continue living, all the while knowing the possibility of sinking into severe depression was not only likely but a foregone inevitability? And the answer to that question? Sam was not sure.

As far as his own health issues were concerned, Sam was plagued by a constant, dull pain in his hip, and he couldn't walk very well. His memory was going, and he was definitely slowing down. His heart was labouring and it seemed like every day he had less and less energy. So, on one hand, things weren't too good.

But...how was his mood? His attitude? How was life in general? He would be the first to tell you that all was good.

187

He enjoyed life. He adored Mary and loved being with her. He loved their kids and grandchildren. He enjoyed reading, bird watching and gardening. He even had an old three-speed bicycle he enjoyed riding from time to time. Not only did the good parts of his life outweigh the bad, they also contributed to his overall emotional well-being, mitigating his aches and pains and lack of energy.

So Sam would be voting no on the end of life issue. Would Mary? He wasn't sure. In fact, after all was said and done today, one thing was certain, they had a lot to talk about.

Just then, from behind, there was a tap on his shoulder, startling him.

"Hi there, Boss Man," Mary chided. "Thinking about that girlfriend of yours again?"

Sam laughed. "How'd you guess?"

She moved in front and held out a small container filled to nearly overflowing with a hot fudge sundae, Sam's absolute favourite. "Surprise. I got you a treat." She grinned as she placed it in his eager hands. She also had a fist full of napkins.

"My God, this is perfect," he told her, using a little red spoon and beginning to dig in. "How'd you guess that this would hit the spot? I've always got room for some ice cream."

"I know. I've got your number, big time, mister." Mary grinned. She sat down next to him and started working on her own treat, a waffle cone the size of her head.

"Salty caramel?" he asked through a mouthful of cold vanilla ice cream and warm chocolate, savouring their combined flavours. He enjoyed watching her tear into her cone. Salty caramel was her favourite ice cream in the entire world.

"Do you even have to ask?" she mumbled, chewing away enthusiastically.

188

Now that he thought about, no, he didn't.

They passed the time chatting and enjoying their ice cream while looking over the lake and marvelling at how scrumptious each bite tasted, their simple pleasures magnified by not only their age but by the very real reason they'd come to spend the night at the Inn.

Every now and then people passed by, either on bikes or walking or jogging. And every now and then someone made eye contact with them and smiled and said, "Hi" and Sam and Mary smiled back and said, "Hi" in return. And none of those friendly folks never once came close to imagining that the two old people sitting peacefully side by side on a park bench in the bright afternoon sun, enjoying their ice cream and talking together, were only a few hours away from deciding whether or not tonight was going to be the night they were going to put an end their lives.

When they finished eating they stood up. Sam stretched his stiff muscles while Mary dumped their trash in a refuse container nearby. Before they left, though, there was one small bit of business to take care of. Since she had playfully snuck up from behind earlier Sam hadn't noticed something else Mary had brought with her, something she had hidden on the ground behind the bench. She now picked it up and showed it to him.

"Look what else I got you, Mr. Gimpy," she said. Sam turned to look just as she proudly held up her purchase. "Do you like it?"

Thinking she had bought a few new books, he was stunned speechless when he saw what she had done. He took a moment to answer because he'd never seen anything like it before in his life. Mary was holding was a beautifully carved wooden cane. It looked like it was crafted from diamond willow, a tree species common to northern Minnesota. Its reddish-brown hue was accentuated by mellow yellow traces of grain running through it. The wood was polished to a gleaming sheen so bright it was glowing in the sunshine.

Mary handed it over and he cradled it in his hands, reverently running his fingers over the wood's smooth surface. His ambivalent and somewhat negative thoughts about using something to assist himself in walking were completely blown away by the beauty and craftsmanship of the cane itself. It was the most gorgeous handmade piece of wood he'd ever seen. Its beauty actually brought a tear of joy to his eye.

"I more than like it," he told her, "I love it." He quickly wiped an eye, his heart touched by his wife's thoughtfulness.

"You're not mad I got it for you, are you?"

Over the five years since his hip replacement they'd talked often about him getting something like a cane to help with his increasingly unsteady walking, his tendency to trip on the tiniest obstruction in his path and his deteriorating heart capacity. He'd won every discussion with immature arguments all cantered in some way shape or form around his stubbornness and close-mindedness.

But after his struggle today to cover the mile and a quarter from the Inn to Fitger's, Sam was now willing to accept his limitations and was amenable to trying anything. The cane was just the ticket. "Not at all," he told her, enthusiastically. "In fact, honestly, I've been thinking about getting a cane off and on all day." He paused and smiled a little sheepishly. "You're a mind reader, is what you are." He shuffled his feet in anticipation and smiled at Mary. "Let's give it a try." He was willing to bet his intuitive wife knew what he'd been thinking all along today.

Mary grinned. "Go for it, Boss Man."

Sam shouldered his day pack and took hold of the

smooth handle. There was a slight curve to it that fit his hand perfectly, almost as if it were made for him. He liked the cane's light weight, yet it also felt solid and strong, like it would last forever. "It's great." He smiled at Mary. "Fantastic, in fact. You did a good thing, here."

She smiled in return. "It's about time you listened to me." She reached into her pocket and took out a clean Kleenex and dabbed the corner of his eye. Then she put it away, not bothering to say a thing.

He reached out and gave her a one armed hug. "Thanks so much for putting up with me."

She smiled. "You're an all right guy sometimes. I just might keep you around."

When Mary joked with him like she was doing now it meant more to him than any declaration of love.

But he couldn't resist saying, slapping the tip of his new cane in his left hand, "Ok. Now, I'll race you. Watch out. One, two, three, go!" And off he shuffled, huffing along with his new cane tapping the way along the path.

Mary pulled up next to him in about four steps. "Calm down there, Speedy Gonzales. We've got all the time in the world to get back to the Inn. Let's just take it easy."

Sam slowed his pace because, like so many other things she'd suggested throughout their life, Mary was correct. They really did have all the time in the world. At least until later tonight when they'd have their discussion about the Our Right to Die Declaration.

Right now though, they would just think about today and the warm late afternoon sun on their faces and their outing together in the fresh air along the rocky shoreline of Lake Superior. And for them that was all that mattered.

Mary took Sam's left arm and they slowly made their way back towards the Inn. The sun was starting to dip into the west over the hills of Duluth and the shadows were lengthening. The air had a crisp coolness to it, making the times they stepped from shadow into sunlight gratefully warming to their old bones and adding to their feeling of happiness from being outdoors and sharing their time together.

They really were in no hurry. They poked along, pointing out purple kale and fragrant herbs planted in tidy, well maintained public gardens near the walking path. Pretty, ten foot tall Amur Maples with their leaves turning burgundy red and flaming orange added more colour to the scene. Fall was their favourite time of year, and the effect of all the colour along the walkway was at the same time both calming and invigorating; the kind of feeling that was fun to experience.

Sam was also enjoying his new found freedom of movement with his new wooden cane, finding he could walk better and at a steadier, less painful pace. The adage concerning the tortoise and the hare, 'Slow and steady, wins the race', came to his mind more than once during their walk, making him grin a little.

It was nearly six in the evening by the time they returned to the Inn. The sun would be completely set in less than an hour. They used their key card to enter through the back door into an open area that would be used tomorrow morning for breakfast seating. As they passed by the front desk Gary waved to them before he turned with a smile to help a middle aged couple check in and they waved back. Mary leaned toward Sam and whispered, "He's such a friendly young man," as they walked by.

They took the elevator to the third floor and walked down the hall. They didn't see another soul, as though they had the whole floor to themselves. Mary led the way, a step or two ahead of Sam and his new cane. After years of struggling with his hip replacement and vain enough not to want to admit he needed assistance, it was his dear wife's intuition to know that all it would take was the right time and right place to push him to do what he should have done years ago. He was glad she did. Plus, there was no doubt in his mind at all; his new handmade cane was really cool.

They entered their room and Sam set his cane aside, fighting the urge to give it a loving pat-pat. *To hell with it*, he thought, hesitating only a moment. Then he did. Mary went about getting settled and finished up by putting a few toiletries out on the counter of the sink.

They both loved The Inn on the Lake and this particular room especially. It was the same room they'd stayed in for each of their thirty-two visits. To the left was a large bathroom and shower with a door that closed for privacy. Next, along the wall, there was a nice sized desk, then a king sized bed, and a cosy sitting area with two comfortable easy chairs. There was a convenient little table between them where they could set mugs of coffee or tea. Immediately next to Sam along the right side of the room was a closet and then a good sized counter and sink. Next was a long, low chest of drawers with a flat screen television on the end nearest the sitting area.

A great feature of the room was a good sized gas fireplace mounted in the wall, which they'd used quite a bit during previous stays, both for the ambiance and for heat. There were also framed prints on the walls capturing scenes associated with the lake; wild waves crashing on the shore, fishing trawlers trolling for whitefish and iron ore ships battling November storms.

But the real draw was at the opposite end of the room from where he was standing; a large picture window overlooking a secluded balcony and beyond it the vast expanse of Lake Superior stretching to the far horizon.

A door to the right of the window led out to the balcony and that's where they went. "Let's sit and enjoy the view," Mary said, settling into one of the comfortable chairs. She motioned to the one next to her. "Come on, Sam. Come and join me."

He really wanted to, but instead asked, "First, should I go back down and get us some hot chocolate?" He was mentally kicking himself for having forgotten to think about bringing up a favourite treat of theirs when they were downstairs. The free hot chocolate provided by the Inn was an added bonus for them.

"No, that's OK," Mary said. "We can make some tea later." She patted the chair next to her. "Come and join me. Let's sit for a while."

Sam appreciated that after over fifty years of married life his wife still wanted to spend time with him. His guess was that not all marriages were like that. He pulled up a chair and sat down. If they leaned forward just a little they could see the boardwalk about seventy five feet away. Past it was a rocky breakwater with waves still rolling in, the gulls dipping and gliding on a light breeze, calling and squawking. To the left they could see the far shoreline where they'd been walking earlier. They could even make out Fitger's if they looked closely.

But it was the wide expanse of water stretching into the distance that took their breath away, just like it did every single time they visited. From their third floor vantage point Lake Superior was a stunning sight, an inland sea, right there in northern Minnesota. They split their time between looking out over the water and watching people stroll along the boardwalk, letting the moments slip by as if their time together was infinite and would last forever.

Over the next hour or so, they both took showers and Sam made them some tea. They spent most of their evening outside on the little balcony, enjoying each other's company and being together. Mary was wrapped up in a blanket to ward off a slight chill. Sam had put on a light jacket. They each had a book, so they read a little, people watched a little and looked at the lake a lot.

At one point, after they'd finished their tea, Sam took his cane and went downstairs to a serving area reserved for guests and fixed them two big mugs of hot chocolate. When he realized he couldn't use his cane and carry two full, steaming mugs at the same time, one of the staff cleaning in the lobby noticed his predicament and asked if he could help. Sam gratefully took him up on his offer, and he was kind enough to bring the hot chocolate out onto the balcony where he set the mugs on the little table. Sam gratefully gave him a five dollar bill for his effort.

Mary sleepily sipped from her mug as Sam fought back the urge to gulp from his. He really was kind of addicted to the Inn's hot chocolate. They talked back and forth as a sense of calm settled over them and they became enveloped in the deepening twilight. The day was winding down and the lights along the boardwalk began to come on. Mary reached over and took Sam's hand. They smiled at each other, at peace with the world.

There was enough light from the room coming through the window that Sam could read. He was so relaxed he'd completely forgotten about the Our Right to Die Declaration.

After a little while he was engrossed in his book when it occurred to him that Mary had suddenly become very quiet. He glanced over just as she let loose with a huge yawn. It had been a long day, and she was obviously tired. In fact it occurred to him that it was completely dark out. Night had fallen.

"Should we go inside?" he asked. "I could turn on the fireplace."

She shivered a little. "That sounds like a good idea. I'd like that."

Mary picked up her blanket and their books while Sam took their now lukewarm hot chocolate. They went inside and Sam lit the fireplace as they got themselves settled. After a few minutes watching the flames flicker, Mary surprised him by asking if he'd like to play a game of cribbage. She seemed to have revived and picked up a bit of energy from her rest on the balcony.

"What do you say, Boss Man, just for old time's sake?"

Sam glanced at her and swore he could detect that same impish twinkle she seemed to have had in her eye all day.

"Sure," he readily agreed, "if you don't mind losing." He grinned, joking with her.

If they'd bothered to keep track over the fifty-three years of their marriage and the thousands of times they'd played cribbage, Mary had won probably eighty-five percent of the games. At least that what it seemed like to Sam. He was always a willing competitor, though, just not very good at cards compared to her.

"I think I can handle it," she laughed, and began shuffling the deck while he set up the board and pegs. When they were all set, and she was just about ready to cut to see who would deal, she stopped dead, set the deck aside and looked at him. "You know, we haven't talked about the Declaration yet. We really should get that out of the way."

Here it comes.

Sam moved the board aside. "You're right. Honestly? I'd been having such a good time this afternoon, I'd completely put it out of my mind." He took a nervous sip from his mug. The hot chocolate was now cold and just short of disgusting. He held up his hand. "Just a second." He went to the microwave, set the mug in and turned it on for a minute. The noise gave him some time to consider

196

what Mary was going to say. Was her decision going to be yes or no?

Sam's guess was that it was going to be no. She'd been having a really good day; she'd enjoyed their walks, and she enjoyed talking with Richard and Gary at the front desk. She'd liked feeding the gulls, she'd had fun talking with Sean at Amazing Grace and then taking their walk along Lake Superior's shoreline. She'd been friendly with people, happy and outgoing all day long. She'd bought them ice cream at Fitger's along with his beautiful new cane.

In short, she'd been on top of the world; a rare place for her to be, but, nevertheless, a place that was certainly possible for her to attain again in the future. At least it'd be something for them as a couple to shoot for. Plus, and the fact couldn't be ignored, Mary was a fighter. Sam was willing to bet she would want to rise to the challenge of living a happy and productive life for another year.

So the way Sam saw it was this: the sleeping pills would stay put away. Mary would want to stay alive and if she did, so did he. Sam would join his wife for another year of living their lives together. There would be no Right to Die Declaration fulfilment tonight at the end of this, one of the most memorable days they'd ever spent at the Inn On the Lake. At least that would be his guess.

Turned out he was right.

He took his mug back and sat down and looked at his wife. Mary's eyes were sparkling merrily as she said, "I won't keep you in suspense, Boss Man. I'm voting no. I'd like another year with you."

A surging flood of relief overwhelmed Sam and his heart leapt with joy. "I'm so glad to hear that." He moved quickly next to her, dropped to his knees and gave Mary a big, warm, all-encompassing hug. "I feel exactly the same way." Words could not describe how happy he felt.

She hugged him back. "So you can put up with me for another year?" She asked, not having to add anything more about her depression and dark moods.

"Obviously, yes," he said into her hair. "I might ask the same, of you." He released her, but kept kneeling next to her. He wanted to be close as possible.

Suddenly, his hands began shaking, his body releasing the stress he'd been under not knowing the outcome to what they'd be deciding. With the decision made, the relief was palpable, as was the happiness that now filled his entire being.

Mary placed her hands in his. At her touch his entire body immediately relaxed. *They were going to have another year together!* Sam was overjoyed. He looked into her eyes and she returned his loving gaze. They didn't have to say a thing.

Unexpectedly, along with the relief, there was also the tiniest bit of a sharp twinge in Sam's heart. *It's probably just the aftermath of the ice cream I had earlier,* he thought, and ignored it. *I'm not going to say anything. I don't want to spoil the moment.*

"Yes I can, Boss Man," she said, finally, in answer to his earlier question. "I want to stay living with you. I wouldn't change a thing." Sam took her words as a good sign that she might actually be winning the overall battle with her depression. At least for now. He was relieved for her, and them. "I'm so very happy," she added and he believed her.

She squeezed his hands for a moment before letting go. Then she hugged him tightly. He hugged her back, lost in her embrace, enjoying how happy he was; how happy they both were.

Unfortunately, after a minute Sam's knees started to give out. They hugged once more and he stood up, wincing

198

as his bones cracked. "Well, in that case," he said, "how about if I dump this old chocolate out and make us some fresh chamomile tea to celebrate?"

"That would be wonderful," Mary said, reaching out and touching his hand once more. "Just perfect."

No further words were necessary. They both knew that their mutual decision to leave the pills untouched and to continue living together for another year had ignited something special between them. Their love, deep already, had just become immeasurably deeper, their bond, immeasurably stronger.

Sam made their tea. Mary opened the bag of cookies from Amazing Grace and they shared them while playing three games of cribbage, Mary beating him two games to one. Neither of them could recall ever having such a wonderful evening.

By the time they finished playing cards, Mary was yawning almost nonstop. The day, spectacular as it was, had completely worn her out. She stood up and stretched. "I'm going to go brush my teeth and get ready for bed, Boss Man. Maybe read a little. You go ahead and stay up if you want."

She knew him well. Sam was still a little wound up from the day, and, more specifically, the evening. They'd have another year together; he was overjoyed and didn't want the day to end. "Sounds good," he smiled at her. "I think I might go out on the deck and listen to the lake for a while."

When she was ready and had crawled under the covers Sam sat down next to her and made like he was tucking her in, joking with her a little. She shooed him away, laughing. They kissed lightly.

"I love you, Mary," Sam said.

"I love you, too," she smiled, caressing his cheek.

Sam stood and left Mary to her book, but she was so tired she immediately began dozing off. The bedside clock read a little after ten and he didn't want to bother her, so he turned off the fireplace and all the lights in the room except for her bedside lamp. The he grabbed his jacket and a blanket and made his way as quietly as he could out onto the balcony.

At that hour, the boardwalk was quiet. He only saw a few walkers, a jogger and one or two couples strolling hand in hand. The lights along the walkway resembled old time street lamps from Victorian England, and they cast a pleasant glow, illuminating the ground softly and adding to the almost poetic beauty of the scene.

There was no moon, so the sky was pitch black and Sam could see a white wash of stars above the lake. He'd checked the Duluth Shipping News before they'd left home and knew that a cargo ship was expected sometime later this evening. He casually scanned the dark horizon, looking for the ship's lights. The W. J. McCarthy was a one-thousand foot ore boat on its way to Duluth Harbor from Sioux St. Marie. He thought that it would be fun to see the huge vessel come across the lake, making for port through the canal nearby and into the harbour just beyond. For now, though, the lake was void of any ship's lights and was as deep and dark as a bottle of India ink.

He was wrapped up in the blanket to stay warm and must have dozed off. A sudden gust of cold wind startled him. It pierced his blanket and caused a chill to rush deep into his bones. He shivered and felt goose-bumps run up and down his arms. Coming wide awake, he checked his pocket watch and saw he'd been asleep for twenty minutes. Maybe it was his shivering that caused what happened next to happen, but suddenly he got a sense of grim foreboding. His entire being went on high alert and he became overwhelmed with the strangest feeling. *Something's not right.* He immediately thought of Mary. She'd been overly tired. She'd gone to bed earlier than they normally did. She'd been yawning all evening. *Was something going on with her? Was something happening to her that he should have noticed and been aware of, but wasn't?*

Then he had a thought, a horrible realization. It hit him so hard, panic set in and his heart started to race. The Right to Die Declaration! Those sleeping pills! Had she not been truthful with him earlier that evening when they'd talked? Had she lied to him about wanting to continue living with him to spare his feelings? Had she, in fact, really taken those pills? Shit!

He jumped up from his chair, knocking it and the table over as he scrambled to reach for the door handle. He needed to check on her. Fast. Images raced through his mind, each worse than the next, until he was left with the worst scenario imaginable; Mary lying comatose in the bed slowly succumbing to the effects of those damn sleeping pills.

Sam yanked open the door and at that exact moment his heart thumped like it was turning over on itself. He clutched at his chest as he looked into the room. The bedside lamp was still on. He could see Mary lying there, turned away from him, blankets pulled tightly around her. She looked so peaceful. Was she asleep, or...

He took a step towards her and suddenly his heart slammed into overdrive. It felt like it was being plummeted by a sledge hammer. He pressed down on his chest thinking he might be able to slow it down, but he couldn't. It only raced faster. Faster. Faster. *Oh, my god. What's happening?* He only had one answer. He was having a...

In the next instant his heart exploded. The pain was so overwhelming it knocked him to the floor. He rolled into a foetal position as sweat poured out of every pore in his body. He was having trouble breathing. It felt like he had a hundred pound weight on his chest, bearing down, pressing him into the carpeting. The pain was unimaginable. He was afraid he might vomit.

He panicked and tried to fight back, tried to rid his body of the agony and regain his equilibrium, but he was losing the battle. He felt himself start to pass out but fought to stay conscious. His mind was racing. *I need to get to Mary. I need to see if she is still alive. I need to convince myself that she hasn't taken those sleeping pills. She wouldn't leave me, would she? She wouldn't take her own life, would she? Not after how happy she was today.*

He tried to call to her but couldn't form any words. His mouth was numb. His mind was going blank. He was losing all control of himself and the thought formed: *Is this what it's like to die?*

With one supreme last effort he tried to crawl to Mary thinking, *I've got to see her.* He forced himself across the carpet. Ten feet, five feet. He inched his way, dragging himself along with his right arm, using his elbow for leverage.

It took what seemed like forever. Finally he made it to the edge of the bed. He reached up and grasped the mattress with his right hand, the one hand that seemed to be working. He tried to raise himself up to her. He wanted to touch her. To gain strength from her. To see if she was still alive.

With a last resolve and building up strength he didn't know he had, Sam pulled himself up until he was eye level with Mary's shape under the covers. His vision was blurry and he wasn't able to focus. There was a fog in his eyes, a mist. He couldn't do anything other than blink rapidly and hope that his vision cleared. The pain in his chest was unrelenting and he fought to stay conscious.

Suddenly his sight returned. For the briefest of moments, Mary's form came into view. He could see her clearly, and when he did, he saw what he needed to see. The blanket she was wrapped in rose and fell, then rose and fell again. She was breathing. And it was steady and strong. She hadn't taken the sleeping pills. Sam was overwhelmed. His dear wife was still alive.

The bliss of that moment was lost in the next instant when everything changed. His vision left him, going cloudy and steadily out of focus. The pain in his chest accelerated until it was beyond unbearable. It was crushing him. He couldn't stand it anymore. He could barely make out Mary's form under the covers. He wanted to touch her so badly. He forced his hand forward. Then, with one final push, he was there. He could touch her! Oh, the joy! He wanted to continue living with her so badly. They had so much left to share with each other. So much life.

But no. Sam slowly slumped to the floor. He couldn't get up. Couldn't move. He began drifting, drifting away. He fought to stay conscious. *Please let me stay. Please let me live. Please, please, please.*

He struggled to come back, fighting to reach out to Mary, but he was losing. Darkness was setting in. *No,* Sam was thinking. *I don't want to leave. I'm not ready to go. Not now. Please let me stay. Please.*

But, the darkness deepened. *Oh, no. I don't want to go away. Please. Please. I'll do anything. Anything, because anything is better than this. Anything is better than my life with Mary...*

being...

...all...

...over.

Then final darkness. Sam was gone.

Later that night, Mary awakened and looked at the clock. It read two-twenty. She stretched and rolled over, feeling wonderfully refreshed, wondering where Sam could be. He was definitely not in bed. She looked across the room to the door leading to the deck. Odd. It was open. *No wonder it's so cold in here*, she thought to herself. *Why did Sam leave it open?*

Sam. Sam! She bolted up right, clutching at her chest, wondering where he was. *Did his memory fade and he forget where he was? Did he wander off and was now lost somewhere?*

Her eyes frantically searched the room. When she didn't see him, her panic rose until she happened to glance down and saw him lying on the floor next to the bed, his arm stretched out towards her. She slid down and took him in her arms, holding and rocking him. He was limp, unresponsive. Smoothly shifting into her nursing mode Mary felt Sam's neck for a pulse. There was none. In that moment she realized the awful reality. She'd dealt with enough death at the hospital to know without a doubt that Sam was gone, passed from this life forever.

What happened? Oh, Sam. Oh, my dear, dear husband. Her mind raced, searching for answers. She held him tighter, as tears formed and ran down her cheeks. *He must have had a massive heart attack*. It was the only answer she could think of that made sense. She tried to will her strength into his body, wanting desperately to bring him back from where he was, but it didn't help. His limp unresponsiveness said it all, and Mary was forced to accept the awful truth; Sam was dead and gone forever.

With that awful realization, Mary broke down, her body racked with sobs, her soul crushed. She lost track of time as she cradled her husband's head in her arms, holding him to her bosom, quietly weeping over the loss of her Sam, the good man whom she had loved so dearly and for so many years.

Nearly an hour went by before Mary was finally able to bring herself back to the here and now. She knew that the right thing to do was to call 911 emergency and report her husband's passing. The paramedics needed to come to the room, examine his body and verify that his heart had quit beating. A doctor needed to pronounce him dead.

Beyond those legally mandated activities, the police would probably even need to question her. After all, Sam had died while she was in the room with him and police involvement was a common procedure in those kind of cases. In short, people in charge of such things needed to take over.

Right. Yes. Those are the immediate things she needed to do, she told herself. However, they were all just the cold logistics required by law. More importantly, for Mary, what she really needed was to begin to take the first tiny steps forward in learning how to accept the loss of her husband. She needed to figure out how she was going to move on with her life.

Mary closed her eyes to gather strength. There were so many things that she was supposed to do and take care of, but she did none of them. Instead, she continued to hold onto Sam, rocking him in her arms.

After a while, she put into place a plan of her own.

She looked at the clock on the bedside table. It read three-fifteen. *Good*, she smiled to herself. *There was plenty of time*. She moved away from her husband, laying him gently on the carpet. Then she stood and went about the room turning on lights so she could see better. Next she went to her travel bag and took out her bottle of pills. She obtained this particular bottle years ago when she worked at the hospital, long before regulations were made more restrictive. These pills were strong. She knew their dosage. She knew they would do the job.

Mary went to the sink and looked at her image in the mirror. *Do I really want to do this*, she asked herself? *I have my children and grandchildren to think about. How will this affect them?* She knew her death would be traumatic for her loved ones, especially on top of the loss of Sam, her children's loving father. But she was old and going to die someday anyway. Sam already had. Death was a necessary part of life. Somewhere along the way in her children's grieving process, they would come to the conclusion that both of their parents had lived full and useful lives; their deaths, though sad, were certainly inevitable.

Mary took a sheet of paper from the desk and quickly wrote, "I'm sorry kids but I just couldn't go on living without your father. I hope someday you will understand."

It was not their lives she had to face now, but her own; her life without Sam, her Boss Man, by her side. It was a life she didn't want to live. The truth of the matter was that the time was right. The time was now.

Mary shook out the number of pills she calculated years ago would be the required amount and added two more. She put them in her mouth and washed them down with a drink of water from the faucet. She had about fifteen minutes before they began to take effect.

She moved through the room tidying things up. She straightened the covers on the bed. She used a towel to wipe down the sink and carefully hung it on the rack. She made sure the towels in the shower were straightened and hanging evenly. She rinsed the mugs they used and set them to dry upside down on a wash cloth on the counter. She closed the book she was reading and set it on the nightstand. She found Sam's book and did the same on his side of the bed. When she was done she looked around, happy with what she saw. She didn't want whoever found them to think they were slobs.

In scanning the room, her eyes fell upon the picture window overlooking the lake. She looked through it to the black night beyond. Starting to feel drowsy she made her way to the door leading outside and stepped onto the balcony. The air was brisk and momentarily revived her, but it would take more that cold air blowing in off Lake Superior to bring her back. If fact, nothing would. Not now. In a few more minutes her body would start to shut down. She would fall asleep, and her major internal organs would slowly cease to function. Finally her heart would stop and, within five minutes, she would be gone. Just like Sam.

Mary straightened up the chairs on the deck that Sam knocked over and set the little table between them. She folded the blanket and set it on one of the chairs. *There*, she said to herself, *it looks good. Neat and tidy*.

She turned to look at Lake Superior. Due to the darkness she could barely make it out, but the lake was certainly there, like it had been for ten thousand years. She took heart in knowing it would still be there after she was gone, a living memorial, if you will, a testament to her and Sam's love.

Mary took a last long moment and listened. She didn't have to strain; she could hear the waves breaking rhythmically on the rocks nearby. It was a sound both she and Sam had loved ever since they began coming to the Inn. She left the door cracked a few inches and went inside. If she was lucky, she would be able to hear the waves when she lay down next to her beloved husband.

Before she did that, however, there were a couple of things left to do. She took her phone and Sam's and opened up the backs and took the batteries out, disabling them. Then she went to the door leading to the hallway and placed a Do Not Disturb sign on the outside handle. Then she set the deadbolt. No one would find them until the afternoon at the earliest, and she'd be long gone by then. The last thing she did was to go to Sam's backpack. She reached inside

207

and removed the Our Right to Die Declaration. It was only a few pages long and didn't take a minute for her to tear it into small pieces. Then she flushed them down the toilet. In a minute the Declaration was gone for good.

Stumbling slightly, she turned off all the lights except for the one by her side of the bed. She was now ready to lie down next to Sam. But before she did, she had a thought. She looked around and then saw what she was looking for; Sam's new cane was propped up against the wall near the table where they'd played cribbage. She reached for it and held it in her hands. She smiled at the memory, just a short while ago, of how much he had appreciated her gift. She ran her hands over the beautifully smooth wood and then placed it reverently next to him.

Next she moved him onto his back, just like she'd done for countless other bodies she'd prepared for viewing when she worked at the hospital. She was gentle with him, this man she had loved her entire life. This man who was, in his own way, as much a part of her life as she was of his. The two of them together, she knew, formed the absolute truth of their marriage; together they made each other whole.

Finally she lay down. Earlier she'd removed a comforter from the chest of drawers and now she pulled it over the two of them. She was so sleepy...so very sleepy. She curled up next to Sam and put her head on his chest, something she'd done thousands of times before during their long marriage. Their marriage. Words couldn't begin to describe how wonderful it had been being married to Sam. It had been so much, much, more than she had ever hoped it would be.

She snuggled closer to him and closed her eyes. The room was quiet, so peaceful and still. She could hear her heart beating, hear it slowing down. She was beginning to lose consciousness. And then, just before sleep overtook her, the last sound Mary would ever hear made its way into the room and its presence known, sent on a breeze blowing softly off the lake, the rhythmic sound of the waves of Lake Superior, breaking against the rocks nearby, lapping against the shoreline. They were calling her home.

She smiled at the memories the sound of the waves brought. Then she began drifting...drifting...drifting away.

Finally, sleep overtook her.

And then she heard no more.

A month after the bodies of Sam and Mary were discovered, Gary the desk clerk was sitting at a round table in the Inn on the Lake's small break room. Rick came in through the door and Gary looked up and greeted him.

"Hi."

"Hi, yourself," Rick said. He went to the coffee pot, poured half a mug and sat down next to him. "What 'cha reading?"

Gary showed him the book, a brand new but slightly worn paperback. Rick glanced at it and said, "Never heard of the guy."

"It's pretty good," Gary said and then added, "The old guy who died in 358 last month? He was reading it."

"Really? How do you figure that?"

"Remember I let the police in? I noticed it on the night stand. I thought I'd check it out."

"Any good?"

"Yeah, I like it."

They were quiet for a minute. Rick blew on the coffee and took a sip, thinking Gary might have more to say. He liked the young employee, thought he might even have management potential, so he prompted him, "Weird about them, though, wasn't it? Who would have thought they'd both die on the same night like that?"

"I know," Gary said, carefully marking his place. "I think about it a lot. They seemed like such nice people. I read in the newspaper the cops figured he died of a heart attack and she couldn't handle the grief and took her own life with sleeping pills." He was silent for a minute, thinking. Then he said, "I just don't get it."

"Get what? They were old. Maybe their time had come. Maybe it was supposed to happen."

Gary wasn't convinced. "Do you really believe that? That there is a time and place for everything? Even when you die? What do you call that? Predeterminism or something like that? We studied that kind of thing in my philosophy class up at school." Gary was a liberal arts student at the University of Duluth. He pointed in the direction of the city before continuing, "If that's the case, how do you explain the bottle of sleeping pills they found in her purse? Who carries something like that around with them anyway? And why?"

Gary looked hard at Rick, challenging him to give him an answer.

But Rick had no answer and was suddenly leery of the conversation. Like most people, talking about death was not something he was comfortable doing. "I have no idea," he said, "but I do know this; I plan on living for a long, long time. No sleeping pills for me. No way."

He quickly got up, rinsed the mug in the sink and walked to the door, making a point of checking his watch. "Breaks almost over. It's pretty slow out there. I'll man the counter. See you in a few minutes, okay?"

Gary glanced at his own watch. "Yep. Be right there."

He watched Rick walk out of the door and then tried to go back to his book but was unable to concentrate. He set it aside, thoughts turned inward. He'd been having trouble this past month getting over what happened that night up in room 358. He liked the old guy and his wife. They seemed like nice people. In his backpack he had a copy of the book she was reading, too, written by a female author he'd never heard of. Somehow those two books were making him feel closer to the old couple.

But their death had rattled him that was for sure. It had all happened so fast. One day they were alive and well, vibrant and smiling. Next day, bang, they were gone, just like that. Such a sudden and tragic loss. He just didn't get it. Why did their deaths happen the way they did? And, more to the point, how did it happen that they died together like they did? He just didn't understand.

He held the book in his lap and stared out into space, letting his mind drift, thinking about death and dying, wondering what he'd do if he were in the same situation as the old couple when he got to be their age. Like Rick, he didn't come up with an answer.

In a few minutes he glanced at his watch and realized it was time to go back to work. He put the book in his backpack then hurried through the door to the lobby and up to the check-in counter. Rick went back to his office. Gary watched until his boss closed the door and then glanced towards the big windows nearby that looked out over the lake. He saw that the sky was blue, and the waves were gently breaking on the shore. The serene scene made him think, yet again, of the old couple who died. He felt bad they were gone. He would have liked to have seen them next year and maybe gotten to know them a little better.

But, of course, they wouldn't be returning, and the image of Sam and Mary faded from his mind as he turned to the business at hand. Some new guests had just come in through the front door. They were an elderly couple. The old man was using a cane as they slowly made their way across the lobby. Gary noticed that he was wearing sensible walking shoes and she in hiking boots. The lady entwined her right arm with his left. She was about a foot shorter and when she looked up at him and made a comment, they both chuckled quietly.

Gary, watching, figured it must be some sort of inside joke. They seemed very comfortable and happy with each other, that was for sure. For some odd reason, seeing them together made him feel good. Happy.

"Hi, folks," he said greeting them with a smile as they stepped up to the counter. "Welcome to the Inn on the Lake. How may I help you today?"

"Hello, young man," the old man said. He had a friendly, open smile. It was the end of October and cold outside but he looked warm in his dark blue jacket and Minnesota Twins baseball cap. He leaned his diamond willow cane up against the counter and smiled at the little old lady next to him. She responded by smiling back at him and flipping her long, grey braid outside her own warm looking yellow jacket. The old man turned to Gary and pointed out the nearby window with its view of the boardwalk and the expanse of Lake Superior beyond. He said, "This is our first visit to your Inn. My wife and I would like a room with a view of the lake. One night only. Do you have any available?"

Gary observed the couple with a sort of vague recognition. Had he seen them before? They looked like...but then he shook his head. *No. It couldn't be*, he thought to himself. *No, way. They died last month.* He collected himself and returned a smile. "You bet I do. I've got a nice one for you up on the third floor."

"Did you hear that, Marilyn? They've got a room for us. What do you think? Should we take it?"

Next to the old man, the lady leaned into the conversation. "How exciting. It sounds wonderful, Stanley," she said, looking at her husband and grinning. "I think that'll be just perfect for us. Let's take it."

Gary watched as the old couple made eye contact with each other. *Did something silently just pass between them? Some secret something only they knew the meaning of?* He shook his head, again, clearing it of those kinds of weird thoughts, thinking, *Old people, you just never know what's going on with them.* He folded his hands and waited patiently for their final decision.

Finally, after a few moments, the old man broke eye contact with his wife and looked at Gary, smiled and said, "Well, that's all settled, then. You heard the young lady. One room with a view of the lake. We'll take it."

The Coyote

It was a lazy Saturday morning in the Brentwood Estates. Roland Hathaway sat in his silk bathrobe in the family room, reading the Wall Street Journal and sipping his cappuccino, all the while eyeing a hot buttered croissant. *Life is good*, he was thinking to himself.

He casually looked out of the second story window onto his manicured backyard and his feeling of goodwill disappeared in an instant. "Jesus Christ!" he yelled, slamming down his paper. "Ellen, come in here. Quick! There's a damn coyote on our property."

His nine year old son and eight year old daughter were playing nearby and they ran to see.

"Look, Dad." Lyle pointed. "It's got something in its mouth."

"Ew. Yuck," Emily said, covering her eyes and, then, unable to help herself, looked again.

Ellen hurried into the room. "A coyote? Where is it?"

Roland pointed out of the window. "Right in our backyard. Damn thing. Call animal control. Now. It'll probably start killing everybody's pets." When his wife excitedly peered into the backyard and didn't immediately respond to his orders, Roland barked more loudly, "Hurry up, Ellen. Now! Chop, chop!" He clapped his hands together.

Ellen fought back an urge to tell him off, but stopped herself when she noticed the kids were watching them. She took a deep breath, gritted her teeth and said, "All right. I'll get my phone."

Outside, oblivious to the commotion in the Hathaway house, the lean coyote trotted quickly through the pristine yard, avoiding the swimming pool and tennis court. He knew he'd ranged too far from home, but he'd had to. He was on a hunting trip for his mate and their three young pups. The rabbit he'd killed was his reward, much needed food for his hungry family. But the smell of humans frightened him. A few miles ahead lay the rolling hills that marked the edge of the Minnesota River Valley and his home territory. He trotted faster, the rabbit secure in his mouth. He was sure of one thing – he was never coming back. The scent of humans scared him too much, so he'd stick to hunting in the river valley. That was his home. That's where he belonged.

Ellen took her time walking to the front hall desk where her phone was charging, thinking, *to hell with Roland*. She leisurely unplugged it and did an unhurried search for a number to call. While it rang she walked to a side window and looked outside. When she saw the coyote trotting across their lawn she smiled, thinking: *What a beautiful animal it is. You don't see them too often around the suburbs. Well, never, actually.*

Watching the coyote triggered a sudden, unexpected emotion deep inside her. A pleasant, sensual connection, something she hadn't felt in a long time, not since she'd been a young girl growing up on her parents' farm in central Minnesota. Back then, whenever she'd seen a coyote it had made her happy. Many in her part of the state wanted to kill them on sight, but not Ellen. She was drawn to their graceful beauty and wild spirit. In fact, at one time she'd wanted to become a wildlife biologist to study animals like coyotes, to find ways to help them survive, flourish and live in harmony with humans. That was before she'd met Roland. Back then...well, back then he'd been different to the way he was now.

A voice spoke over the line, interrupting her thoughts, "Animal Control. How may I help you?"

Ellen didn't have to think. "Oh, it's nothing," she

responded, politely. "Sorry to have bothered you." She hung up and watched the coyote gracefully leap over their property line fence and disappear from view. "Be safe," she whispered.

From the family room Roland yelled, "Ellen, damn it. Did you call somebody yet? It's getting away."

Ellen sighed and took a moment, reliving another memory: The time back on the farm when she'd seen a female and two pups running along a gravel road while she was riding her horse. The mother had looked back over her shoulder before leading her young ones into the protection of the nearby underbrush. To this day, Ellen would swear she and the female had made eye contact just before the family had disappeared from view, a primal bond forming between them. It was a moment she'd almost forgotten about. Until now.

Making herself return to the present, Ellen called back, "Don't worry. It's taken care of."

"Good. Now come join me for a croissant. They're delicious."

Ellen sighed again, in no mood to hurry off at his command. Instead, she continued looking out of the window, thinking back to when she'd been a young girl living on the farm, back to when she'd had a connection with coyotes and a sense of wildness in her heart. *Where had it gone,* she wondered. *That wildness? Could I ever get it back?*

A few minutes later Roland yelled, "Ellen, what are you doing? Get back in here."

But he had no way of knowing his wife couldn't hear him.

"Dad, look!" Lyle suddenly exclaimed, pointing out of the window. "It's Mom."

Roland hurried to his son's side and looked. His mouth

gaped open in dismay. He watched as his wife walked calmly across the lawn to their property line. She paused only a moment before nimbly climbing the fence and continuing on through their neighbour's yard.

"Where do you think she's going?" Lyle asked, watching in wonder.

Roland stared out of the window, speechless. Finally, he shook his head, utterly perplexed, and whispered, as if to himself, "I haven't a clue."

Outdoors, Ellen was smiling. She had the sun on her face, the breeze in her hair, and she was happier than she'd been in a long time. As she walked she kept her eyes peeled, looking past Brentwood Estates toward the forested hills of the distant river valley, hoping to catch a glimpse of the coyote. *Just once more,* Ellen thought to herself, walking quicker, before breaking into a spirited trot. *Please let me see that beautiful wild animal just one more time.*

Without thinking she began to run, becoming freer with every step. Just like the wind. Just like the coyote up ahead of her. She smiled to herself and ran faster. She hadn't been this happy in a long time.

Frozen Fingers

The wind howled down the canyon. Above the granite walls the leaden sky leaked snowflakes that swirled around the two figures huddled on their knees against the cold. They needed to get a fire going. Fast. Before it was too late.

"Josh, how are those matches holding up?" Eric asked. He had his gloves off and was blowing on his frozen hands. His fingers were turning white and he was losing all feeling in them. "Can you get that kindling lit?"

"Shit, no," Josh swore, his frosted breath immediately turning to ice, adding to the cake building up on his beard and moustache. "I've got three left and I can't feel my fingers to hold them. Can't feel a damn thing." He blew on his fingers to emphasize his point.

Those were not the words Eric wanted to hear. It was twenty degrees below zero. If they didn't get a fire going in the next few minutes hypothermia would set in and they'd begin the slow agonizing process of freezing to death. He blinked to keep his watering eyes from freezing shut. It didn't help and he rubbed at them to clear his vision.

Next to the two men the rushing water of the Yellow Knife River cascaded over ice covered boulders on its way to Lake Superior ten miles to the east. Eric and Josh had been on a winter hiking trip along the trail that ran high above the river, when the ledge of snow they were on collapsed and they tumbled thirty feet down the steep slope into the frigid water below. In just seconds their heavy winter clothing, Josh's dark blue thermal pants and parka, and Eric's tan Carhartt overalls and insulated jacket were soaked through to their skin. The wet clothing and the numbing cold were a dangerous combination.

They had scrambled out and found a level spot in the snow as they took stock of their predicament. The day packs were lost and Eric had sprained his wrist. Josh had wrapped it as well as he could with a wet scarf, but it didn't help much. One consolation was that the cold helped numb the pain, but that was all. Eric could feel his beard icing up and, with his face getting numb, it was getting hard to speak. He wasn't much help. It was up to Josh to build the fire.

They'd built a small tepee of twigs and pine needles, but a combination of wet stick matches and a wind swirling down the narrow canyon walls made getting the match lit next to impossible. With two matches to go, their prospects were grim.

Eric shuffled on his knees closer to Josh, their heavy clothes forming a barrier from the wind. Then, in a gesture of profound intimacy, he motioned to his friend. "Here, give me your hands."

When Josh balked, Eric said, "Don't give me that macho bull." He motioned again and said, softly, "Here, let me help." Eric took his friend's bare hands in his and, ignoring the pain in his wrist, drew them to his lips and blew on them, warming them with his breath.

The warm air melted the ice on Josh's hands and it dripped onto the snow, freezing immediately. Blood flowed into his fingers bringing them back to life. In minute he could wiggle them. "Hey, man that feels good. They're better." He flexed his hand. "I can feel my fingers, now."

Eric blew one last long breath and then Josh quickly moved his hands away, took the second match and struck it against the side of the match box. Nothing happened. It was too wet. On the second try it broke apart and fell to the snow, useless.

The two men looked at each other. "Here," Eric said. "Give me your hands again."

Eric again cupped his friend's fingers and blew on

219

them, willing warmth into them. Their faces were windblown and red. Their teeth were chattering and their eyes watering so much they kept freezing shut. Their beards were filled with chunks of ice. And they only had one match left.

The sun was setting behind the pine trees lining the rim of the canyon. With the lack of sunlight the cold was settling in deep and hard.

Eric blew on Josh's fingers one last time. "Ready?"

"Yeah." Josh took the last match, resolve set in his eyes. He looked at Eric. "Let's do this."

"Go for it, man."

Josh struck the match. Both men watched, their lives hanging in the balance, as the flame flickered...then faded... then caught.

In spite of ice covered beards and frozen faces they looked at each other and grinned. Then they quickly set about building a roaring fire.

Too Many Masks

Bam! Bam! Bam! "Open up, it's the police."

Oh, shit, thought, Bryan, what have I done now? He got out of bed, stumbled over a shoe and fell to the floor. Shit. He got up cursing his fall and, while he was at it, his hangover. "I'm on my way. Hold on."

"Hurry up," came the voice outside his apartment. Impatient was putting it mildly. The guy sounded mad and pissed off. "We need to talk. Now!"

As Bryan crossed the living room he tried to piece together last night. It was only coming back in fragments. Oh, yeah, the Halloween party. The last party in a long line of parties he'd attended wearing a mask.

Wearing masks. Once he'd gotten in the habit of doing it, it really wasn't all that weird, wearing, say, a Tricky Dick Nixon mask to a party. His friends even thought it was pretty cool, saying, "Man, you are some strange dude, you and your masks. The next party is in two weeks. Will you be there?"

The crowd he hung out with liked weirdness so he was happy to oblige. "Absolutely," he told them. "No problem." It was nice to be well thought of. Besides, it was a perfect opportunity to hide. Put on a mask and be someone different. What was not to like?

For one whole year he'd done that, worn masks to parties and by now had accumulated quite a drawer full of them: a ghoul, Yoda, Frankenstein, Elvis, a unicorn, Tricky Dick Nixon, even a parrot. It had been fun hiding behind whatever mask he'd chosen to wear, acting out and being crazy. But it all had come to a head last night.

He'd gone to a friend's Halloween party wearing a mummy mask he'd bought at a local novelty store and he'd wrapped it in strips from a sheet, which he thought had added a nice touch. Once at the party everyone thought he looked great. Even that lady he'd met, Batgirl. Then they'd started drinking, the two of them, and partying hard. Then this, the aftermath. He couldn't even remember how he'd gotten home, or, for that matter, where his strips of sheet had ended up.

If it had been a nightmare or even a bad dream, that would have been one thing, but it wasn't, it was real, and that made it even worse. He'd awoken in the early dawn, dragged himself from bed and made his way shaking to the bathroom where he'd fallen to his knees and thrown up into the toilet, flushed it and threw up again. Nice way to start the day, he'd thought grimly. What a credit to the human race you are.

Then he'd made his way to the sink where he splashed water on his face. His mouth felt drier than the desert, his swollen tongue stuck to its roof. He took a gulp of water, swirling it around but it barely helped. He swallowed and fought back a dry heave. Then he dared himself to look at the mirror, horrified at what he saw – puffed up face, dark bags under bloodshot eyes, hair a mess. Himself a mess. One more night of drinking. One more day looming ahead hung-over and wasted. He couldn't go on like this. He had to clean up his act. He had to quit pretending and hiding behind a mask and face himself for what he really was – a poor excuse for a human being.

More pounding brought him back to reality. Bam! Bam! Bam! *What was this all about?*

He finally got to the door and opened it, hanging on the frame for balance. "What's up?"

A large policeman with a handlebar moustache stood in the door way, frowning. "We understand you were with a girl last night. We need to talk. She's missing."

Holy shit. He stepped back. "Sure," he said, voice shaking. "Come on in."

The cop was just stepping inside when he received a phone call. He listened for a moment, then said, "Okay. I'm on my way." He turned to Bryan and said, "We don't need you. She's been found. She was at a girlfriend's."

He looked hard at Bryan, then took a quick look at his apartment: dirty clothes on the floor, crusted dishes scattered everywhere, a faint aroma of vomit in the air. He shook his head sadly and said, "A word of advice? You better clean up your act, buddy."

Bryan closed the door and looked back into his disaster of an apartment. The one bright spot was the framed picture of his parents he kept on his desk. It had been taken at his twenty first birthday almost two years ago, just before they'd been killed by a drunk driver on a busy stretch of highway on a local interstate. He owed them better than this.

He noticed his mummy mask on the floor and picked it up. Then he went to his desk, took a pair of scissors from the drawer and methodically cut the mask to shreds. It felt good to destroy it. He had to get his act together and this was the only way he could think of beginning. A plan developed. He reached in the drawer for another mask and started cutting. He'd destroy them all. Then he'd figure out a way to live without them. Hopefully his friends would understand, but if they didn't, too bad. This was something he had to do. It wasn't much but it was a beginning. He felt better already.

Abahoochie Spring

My doctor was at least half my age and very formal and direct, which I liked. He sat next to me in his office and said, "I'm sorry, Alex. The tumour is close to your hypothalamus. It's too dangerous for surgery."

I got the message. "How long?"

"Less than a year."

He talked some more, but I wasn't listening. A year to live. Two things immediately came to mind: First off, I was going to keep the news to myself for as long as I could. Second, I was going to go back to where I'd grown up. Back to Montana.

The doctor's voice droned on, but my mind was already in the mountains, deep in the Stillwater River valley and my earliest memory, back to one summer day when I was five and Mom and Ellen had taken those two men on a trail ride. I remembered the four of them talking:

"We could bottle it," one of them had said.

"Yeah, we'd make a mint," the other added. Both men had taken a quick drink out of the clear mountain stream. "We could call it Abahoochie Spring Water. That's what the little lady called this place, didn't she?" They looked at each other, grinning. "Has a nice ring to it."

Then they turned and looked at the 'Little lady' and their smiles withered.

My mom's friend Ellen was a leather tough third generation Montana rancher. She stared back at them and said, quietly, with a hint of a threat in her voice, "I don't think so."

What Mom and Ellen had thought was a simple sight-seeing trip had turned into much more. The two soft looking men were not interested in taking a leisurely horseback ride into the mountains. No. Instead, they were businessmen from Minnesota on the hunt for new ways to make a quick buck. Like bottling spring water.

"This is my family's land," Ellen added. "I'm taking you both back down the mountain right now. We don't want you coming back again. Ever."

Next to her, Mom nodded her head in agreement. They were both deadly serious. The businessmen took one look at them and knew arguing would get them nowhere. They were right. Mom and Ellen lead them away and the spring stayed hidden to all but a few locals.

I remembered the scene like it was yesterday. Now I had the itch to return. Bad.

A few days after I'd left the doctor's office, I called my son to invite him along. He said, "Sorry Dad. I've got a ton of work at the office. Tell you what, I'll ask Benjamin."

My ten year old grandson and I were as close as could be. Benji didn't bat an eye. I heard him in the background yell, "Tell Grandpa, yes!"

So, later that summer he and I drove west from Minnesota for two days to southern Montana and the eastern slope of the Rocky Mountains, stopping at night at small motels along the way. On the afternoon of the third day we parked at the trail head of Boulder Canyon, shouldered our day packs and hiked the trail that lead us into the Stillwater River valley. I wanted to show him the Abahoochie Spring but my brain tumour had muddled my memory. After an hour of searching, I couldn't find it and I was getting frustrated. I'd been with Mom that day so many years ago but I'd only been five or six at the time. A few years later we'd moved to Omaha so she could take a teaching job and I'd never been back. Until now.

I stopped, took off my baseball cap, wiped my sweaty brow and looked around. In a few moments, my agitation immediately vanished. "Man, I'd forgotten how beautiful it is up here," I said to Benji, smiling, taking a moment to breathe in the clean, sage scented mountain air.

"It sure is." He stood next to me, in awe like me. This was the first time he'd ever been in the mountains.

Overhead, a golden eagle soared. Nearby, the Stillwater River was tumbling over boulders the size of compact cars, the rapids filling the air with a roar that just about drowned out our voices. A windblown river mist settled over us, cooling our skin. The valley was dotted with green pines and golden leaved aspen. It had been carved out millions of years earlier by glaciers and was surrounded by mountain peaks, the highest of which was Granite Peak, at over ten-thousand feet the highest mountain in Montana. Even though it was late August, there was still snow covering the top. Far up the side of the valley, Woodbine Falls cascaded hundreds of feet in silent splendour. The entire scene was breathtaking beyond belief, right down to the female moose and her calf we'd come upon half an hour earlier, during our climb to the spot where we now stood.

Benji took my hand. "Let's go, Grandpa."

He was right. It was mid-afternoon and the sun set fast in the mountains. We had to get a move on.

We hiked for another hour or so, moving up away from the river and along the foot of the mountain. "I'm pretty sure the spring was here somewhere," I said stopping and gazing at the rocks, gravel and pine needles that covered the floor of the forest that we had begun walking through. Frankly, I was starting to curse my lack of memory. I didn't see any indication of anything even remotely resembling a spring. Nothing.

Benji had a quicker eye than me. It took him less than a minute to find the percolating stream about fifty feet further up ahead. "Here it is, Grandpa!" he called out, bending down and looking behind at some fallen logs stacked up against a granite boulder. "Look."

I hurried to him and there it was, bubbling out from the ground, framed by a few small boulders, a crystal clear rivulet trickling along a narrow winding path on its way to Woodbine Creek and then to the river.

Excited, he asked, "Can I taste it?"

The pristine water came right out of the ground and had no way of becoming contaminated. "Sure," I said. "I'll join you."

I crouched next to him and we cupped our hands and drank. As we did, it all came back to me, how wonderful the spring water tasted, as cold and sweet and pure as the mountain glaciers that produced it.

I turned to my grandson. "This will be our secret," I told him. "Just the two of us, okay?"

He smiled a smile as wide as the deep blue Montana sky above us. "You can trust me, Grandpa."

I hugged him. "I know I can."

On the hike back, the shadows of aspens and pines lengthened as the sun set behind the mountains. Benji put his hand on my arm to stop me and asked, "Grandpa, can we come back here someday? I'd really like that."

I didn't have the heart to tell him the truth. Instead, I smiled. "Sure," I said. "Absolutely." Who knew? Maybe I'd still be alive next year and would be able to fulfil his wish. After a day like today, I was willing to believe in anything, even that I could live for a long, long time, no matter what the doctor said.

"Next time we'll explore further up the river. How's that sound?"

"Sounds good to me," he said.

We hiked on, the aroma of sagebrush and pine needles filling our senses. We were quiet, soaking up the scenery and letting the cool, fragrant mountain air drift over us, working its magic. Soon the peaceful trickling of the Abahoochie Spring faded into the background, lost to the wind whistling down the granite walls of the canyon. Lost, but never forgotten. By either of us.

About the Author

Jim lives in a small town twenty miles west of Minneapolis, Minnesota. He has held many jobs in his life, the longest being twenty years as a course developer and training instructor for a large manufacturing company. His stories and poems have appeared online in *CaféLit, The Writers' Cafe Magazine, Cabinet of Heed, Paragraph Planet, Nailpolish Stories, Ariel Chart, Potato Soup Journal, Literary Yard, Spillwords (Dec, 2019, Author of the Month), The Drabble, The Academy of the Heart and Mind, World of Myth Magazine, The Horror Tree, The Terror House* and *Bindweed Press.* In print publications: *A Million Ways, Mused Literary Journal, Gleam Flash Fiction Anthology #2,* the *Portal Anthology* and the *Glamour Anthology* by Clarendon House Publishing, *The Best of CaféLit 8* and 9 by Chapeltown Publishing, the *Nativity Anthology* and the *Mulling It Over Anthology* by Bridge House Publishing, *Forgotten One's Drabble Anthology* by Eerie River Publishing, *Gold Dust Magazine, Down in the Dirt Magazine, cc&d magazine, Personal Bests Journal, Nothing Ever Happens in Fox Hollow Anthology,* and the *Oceans Anthology and the 20/20 Anthology* by Black Hare Press. He was nominated for the 2021 Pushcart Prize by The Zodiac Review for his flash fiction story, *Aliens.* His collection of flash fiction and drabbles is scheduled to be released in 2021 by Chapeltown Books. His dysphoria novella *Something Better* will be released in early 2021 by Paper Djinn Press. You can also check out his blog to see more of his stories:

www.theviewfromlonglake.wordpress.com

Like to Read More Work Like This?

Then sign up to our mailing list and download our free collection of short stories, *Magnetism*. Sign up now to receive this free e-book and also to find out about all of our new publications and offers.

Sign up here:
   http://eepurl.com/gbpdVz

Please Leave a Review

Reviews are so important to writers. Please take the time to review this book. A couple of lines is fine. Reviews help the book to become more visible to buyers. Retailers will promote books with multiple reviews. This in turn helps us to sell more books... And then we can afford to publish more books like this one.

Leaving a review is very easy. Go to https://smarturl.it/7uzvrf, scroll down the left-hand side of the Amazon page and click on the "Write a customer review" button.

Read More of Jim's Work in These Books

The Best of CaféLit 8
Published by Chapeltown Books

Order from Amazon:

Paperback: ISBN 978-1-907335-76-1
eBook: ISBN 978-1-910542-46-0

The Best of CaféLit 9
Published by Chapeltown Books

Order from Amazon:

Paperback: ISBN 978-1-910542-54-5
eBook: ISBN 978-1-910542-55-2

Nativity
Published by Bridge House

Order from Amazon:

Paperback: ISBN 978-1-907335-76-1
eBook: ISBN 978-1-907335-77-8

Other Publications by Bridge House

Mulling It Over

edited by Debz Hobbs-Wyatt and Gill James

The Island of Mull, covered in mulls. To mull a drink. An important instrument for making a book. Plenty to mull over here. And plenty to make you think.

As ever, the interpretation has been varied: the Island of Mull, thinking about things, often quite deeply, the odd mulled drink and even something used in making a book - how appropriate again. You will find a variety of styles here and an intriguing mix of voices. There is humour and pathos, some hard-hitting tales and some feel-good accounts. All to be mulled over.

"The Island of Mull is a great concept - we all have had plenty to mull over in 2020. It's a great collection of stories. Very well done!" (*Amazon*)

Order from Amazon:

Paperback: ISBN 978-1-907335-93-8
eBook: ISBN 978-1-907335-94-5

Whisky for Breakfast

by Christopher P. Mooney

The thirty-five stories in Mooney's debut are dominated by a cast of characters who colour outside of society's lines. They are hustlers, prostitutes, addicts, gangsters, killers, thieves, beasts. They are the dangerous, the lost, the lonely, the sick, the suicidal, the broken-hearted. Men and women, defeated by life. Their depravity is real, yet the writing in this uncompromising collection of transgressive fiction, always carefully crafted, evokes the sense that their humanity is not yet lost. In *Whisky for Breakfast*, nothing is off limits.

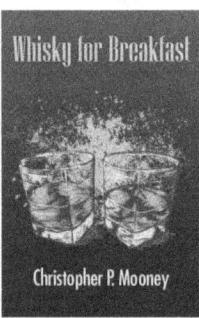

"A terrific read, often shocking and full of memorable characters. This is an excellent collection of short stories and would highly recommend." (*Amazon*)

Order from Amazon:

Paperback: ISBN 978-1-907335-89-1
eBook: ISBN 978-1-907335-90-7

In Fields of Butterfly Flames

by Steve Wade

Ostracised by betrayal, isolated through indifference, gutted with guilt, or suffering from loss, the characters in these twenty-two stories are fractured and broken, some irreparably. In their struggle for acceptance, and their desperate search for meaning, they deny the past. Some abandon responsibility, others are running from something or someone. Some flee their homes and their homelands, while others return home, only to find themselves even more marginalized and estranged.

"It's not too often when a book can make you physically react to the words. Haven't read anything as visceral, gripping and real as this in a long time... Highly recommend!" (*Amazon*)

Order from Amazon:

Paperback: ISBN 978-1-907335-87-7
eBook: ISBN 978-1-907335-88-4

Matters of Life and Death

by Philip M Stuckey

Matters of Life and Death is a collection of stories that examines, in different ways, the many insecurities we experience whilst navigating our way towards the inevitable. Whether it is a fear of the unknown, the burden of loss, or the joy of first love, each of us shares a meandering journey of the unexpected that ultimately defines who we are and how we connect with the universe that created us.

"Varied, deep and interesting, I enjoyed every story. Highly recommended." (*Amazon*)

Order from Amazon:

Paperback: ISBN 978-1-907335-85-3
eBook: ISBN 978-1-907335-86-0

www.ingramcontent.com/pod-product-compliance
Lightning Source LLC
Chambersburg PA
CBHW072230170626
46813CB00003B/1157